THE GUNSMITH

434

The Butcher of the Bayou

THE GUNSMITH

434

The Butcher of the Bayou

J.R. Roberts

SPEAKING VOLUMES, LLC
NAPLES, FLORIDA
2018

The Butcher of the Bayou

ISBN 978-1-62815-756-7

Chapter One

Clint Adams was never one to refuse a free dinner. When that dinner was a thick cut of beef, a heap of potatoes and all the beer he could drink, it was even better.

Alban was a town in Louisiana that was full of good things to eat, drink and smell. A small port on the Mississippi River, Alban had a little bit of everything acquired from places all along the largest watery trade route in the country.

But food and drink weren't the only things of interest to be found there. Along with the goods imported down the river, there were sailors from all around the world who were brought to that spot by ships bound for anywhere a man could imagine. While it wasn't nearly as big as New Orleans, Alban seemed even more chaotic because of everything going on within its borders. Like a painting with more colors than its frame could handle, it was a lot to look at and nearly impossible to take in.

Clint Adams chewed on the last bit of steak from his plate, savoring the perfect texture and the way it mixed with the potatoes that had also been on his fork. He shook his head, unable to come up with the words needed to describe his contentment.

The man sitting across from him at the table laughed and hoisted his beer mug. Scott Meyer was a short fellow with a thick build and a bald head. His face was covered in dark stubble, which matched the roughness of his rumpled clothes.

"I'll be damned, Clint. If I didn't know better, I'd swear you were about to propose marriage to that cut of meat."

After swallowing just enough to get his words out, Clint replied, "That's not a bad idea."

"Probably the beer talking, my friend."

"Could be, but I'm not about to complain."

"And here I thought you'd be more interested in the sights around here," Scott said while glancing over his shoulder.

Clint had indeed been enjoying the sights within the restaurant throughout most of his meal. The Tres Bouchet may not have been lavishly decorated, but it did have plenty of beauty within its sun scorched walls. Most of that beauty came from the young women who served the food while dressed in matching bodices that put their ample assets on display.

The woman serving Clint's table had shoulder length, dark red hair and a friendly smile. Her breasts were pert and smooth, but she looked even better when she turned around. Her hips were wide and round, forming a backside with more than enough curves to entice any man. More than once, Clint found himself distracted by the simple motions of her body as she walked from one side of the restaurant to the other.

"I have no idea what you're talking about," Clint lied unconvincingly.

Smirking, Scott shouted, "Hallie! Get over here!"

The redhead perked up as she smiled and strutted over to their table. "Ready for dessert?" she asked.

"Some of us more than others, I think," Scott chided.

She grinned knowingly, but her eyes drifted over to Clint as she asked, "What would you like?"

"What've you got?"

"Apple pie, raspberry pie and some cake I think."

"What about something stronger to drink?" Scott asked.

"All we have is beer," Hallie replied. "But the saloon next door serves all kinds of imported whiskey."

"Does it, now?"

"I'm not one for whiskey," Clint said.

Lowering her chin a bit, Hallie looked at Clint as if they were the only two souls inside that restaurant.

"Well, if you can wait until I'm done working tonight, I can take you there myself."

"That sounds interesting," Clint said.

"It certainly can be," she told him in a voice dripping with honey.

Both of them watched Hallie walk away. Once she was out of their sight, the two men at the table were able to focus on something else. They got back to their meals for a short while before Scott said, "We have real business to discuss."

"Can't it wait?" Clint groused.

"It's waited long enough. After all, why do you think I brought you out to Louisiana in the first place?"

"Because I saved your life in Oklahoma two years ago?"

"I appreciate that, but no," Scott replied.

"What about Tennessee?"

"What about it?"

"I loaned you fifty dollars to stay in that poker game long enough for your luck to turn," Clint reminded him. "And when those two brothers accused you of cheating, I rolled my sleeves up and stood by your side until the fight was over."

"Not that either," Scott said. "Also, it's not polite to throw favors that you're owed into someone's face."

"I know. That's why I wasn't going to mention that fracas in Arkansas."

"Good lord, Clint! Do I really get myself into that much trouble? I forgot all about Arkansas."

"So, what's got you all worked up this time?" Clint asked. "Must be big if you thought you needed to butter me up with steak and beer before telling me about it."

Leaning forward, Scott said, "It's big, Clint. It's really big."

Chapter Two

Not everyone in Alban was out that night to drink or gamble. Some of the folks walking the streets lived there and were simply trying to get home. For them, the wild music that played was just as natural as the cicadas creaking in the distance. The drunks sleeping along the side of the streets were as much a part of the scenery as trees swaying in the wind.

Two such locals walked quickly past a row of saloons while only nodding politely to a few of the revelers along the way. The man was in his late fifties and had a thick head of salt and pepper hair. He was taller than most and had a face that reflected many years of hard work. The woman beside him had her graying hair pulled back into a bun and a wool shawl drawn tightly around her stooped frame.

Once the saloons were behind them, they slowed their pace and smiled at each other. Clasping his wife's hand a bit tighter, the tall fellow looked down at her and said, "What would you say to a piece of cake?"

"I would say 'pleased to meet you' and then introduce it to my stomach."

The little joke wasn't all that funny, but the old man laughed anyway. He thought plenty of what she said was amusing, which explained a good deal of their happiness for the last few decades they'd spent together. Squeezing her hand a little tighter, he said, "If we head over to Farley's place, we should be able to get some of that chocolate cake they had on special over there."

Her blue eyes sparkled. "Did it have sweet frost?"

"I believe so."

"Then I don't see how we could refuse!"

They made their way to the corner, turned left and continued on through a much quieter part of town. A conversation arose between them which was really about nothing at all. Even so, it consumed their attention until they were within sight of the restaurant marked by a small sign that read "Farley's".

Before the couple could step onto the boardwalk in front of the place, a man stepped out of the restaurant. He was dressed in a plain black suit with a waistcoat that was just a little too big for his slender build. Wiping at the corner of his mouth with the back of his hand, he looked up at the starry sky and pulled in a deep, contented breath.

"Nice night, isn't it?" the old gentleman asked.

The well-dressed customer from the restaurant looked at the couple in front of him, blinked and nodded. "It certainly is."

Raising her eyebrows and showing the slender man a warm smile, the woman asked, "Is there any cake left?"

The stranger winked and nodded. "Not a lot, but there's at least two pieces left."

"Thank goodness," she said.

Tapping his finger to his temple in a casual salute, the old man held his wife's hand to make certain she mounted the boardwalk steps without incident. The slender gentleman stepped aside and held the door open as the two folks approached.

"I don't suppose you could do me a favor?" the younger man said.

"Depends on what it is," the old man replied.

"I'm in town delivering a crate to a friend of mine. It's not a heavy load, but the crate is long and unwieldy. When I arrived, my knot came loose and caused the damn thing to slide off my buckboard. I was hungry and in a foul mood, so I left it where it landed and went to have my supper."

"You need help getting it back onto your wagon?" the old man asked.

"I do," the younger fellow said apologetically. "I wouldn't ask, but the work would take no time at all with a man on either side of the crate."

"My knees ain't what they used to be," the old man said. "Half the time, I can barely lift myself off my bed. Perhaps I could get one of the younger lads inside to give you a hand?"

The man in the waistcoat shook his head quickly. "Don't bother. Like I said, it's a light load. I'll just put it back and tie it down. Serves me right for being in such a hurry the first time around."

The old couple watched the younger man step down from the boardwalk and make his way to the nearest alley where several horses and small wagons were tied. The old man was now holding the door open and he motioned for his wife to step inside. She took a few steps in that direction, paused and then looked up at him.

"He seems like a nice young man," she said.

"Yes, he does."

"Very nice, Miles."

The old man sighed and let the door close. "If that crate is too heavy, I won't be much help to him at all."

"That's true. Let's have our cake."

But the seed had already been planted. Miles was a caring, generous sort and his wife knew that all too well. Hearing the sounds of grunting and struggle coming from the alley was just enough to seal the deal for him.

"Go on inside and get the cake, darling," Miles said. "I'll be along shortly."

She smiled and patted him on the cheek. "You'll get the biggest piece for being such a Good Samaritan."

Miles hitched up his pants and went into the space between the restaurant and its neighbor. His voice could be heard, mingling with the younger man's in what seemed like friendly conversation. She heard the sounds of something heavy being dropped, followed by silence.

After a few moments, she said, "Miles? Are you all right?"

The woman wanted to go inside, but wasn't about to leave her husband in the event that his knee gave out again and he was in pain. She knew a few tricks to get him walking again as well as where to find the doctor at any time of day. She hurried to the wide alley, hoping she didn't find a scene similar to the one that had awaited her when Miles fell off the ladder trying to hang a picture over their fireplace.

When she got to him, Miles was still on his feet. He was being held up by the younger man who gripped Miles's shirt and stared directly into his eyes. The young man's other hand was balled into a fist and wedged against Miles's stomach.

"Leave him be!" the woman said.

Snapping his gaze over to her, the young man shoved Miles away. The man's hand was still a fist, but it wasn't empty. His long fingers were wrapped around the handle of a knife. Its slender blade emerged from Miles's abdomen, trailing thick ribbons of blood along with it.

The woman's eyes were wide with horror. For a moment, she couldn't move or make a sound. That moment passed when she watched her husband's lifeless body drop to the ground like so much refuse. She sucked in a desperate breath, spun around and bolted for the mouth of the alley. She made it less than two steps before she felt an iron grip close onto the back of her neck.

"I wasn't sure you would come when I asked you to," the man said behind her. His breath seeped into her ears like sap dripping from a cracked branch. "Thought I'd have to make do with what I could find."

She was yanked away from the opening leading to the street, just as another couple of people rounded the corner on the other side of the restaurant. The woman opened her mouth to scream. When the first bit of her voice escaped her lips, the man behind her slammed her face against the closest wall.

A series of blows rained down on her. Kicks, punches, knees, all of them pounding into the woman's frail ribs until it was all she could do to prop herself up on all fours. When she tried to look up, a bony fist cracked against her eye. Sobbing, she thought about laying down to play dead in the hope that it might shift the younger man's focus away from her. Instead, his fingers dug into the bun of hair at the back of her head, lifting her up until her neck ached.

"Look," the young man snarled. "Look at what I did."

Along with the limp body of her husband, she could see the body of a woman sitting propped against the wheel of a wagon. She recognized the woman as one of the soiled doves working the town's saloons. Her throat was sliced open and her eyes stared blankly out at the cruel world that had treated her so terribly.

"What do you call this?" the young man hissed. "An embarrassment of riches? I thought you two were too smart to come in here and then I find this bitch right here asking if I wanted her to suck my cock. Soon as I cut her, the old man comes along. Soon as I gut him, you stop by. I must truly be blessed."

"Who are you?" the woman gasped. "What do you want?"

"Does it matter?"

Her eyes darted back and forth between the ground and the man who kept a solid grip on her hair. Whenever she tried to struggle, the younger man wrenched her head to one side as though he was about to wring a chicken's neck. The smell of blood hit her nose and seeped all the way down the old woman's throat. That brought tears to her eyes as she fully realized that her beloved Miles was no more.

"I'm not going to hurt you," the man said.

"Please, let me go," she begged. "I promise I won't tell anyone what happened. Just let me go."

"Sure." The man released the woman's bun, took half a step back and then brought his other hand up to drive his blade straight into the spot where her chin met her neck.

The old woman dangled there, gulping and twitching.

The younger man watched.

Chapter Three

Hallie had offered to bring dessert to Clint and Scott's table. When she mentioned cake, Scott insisted that she bring the entire thing. It wasn't until the cake arrived that Scott would even consider broaching the subject of his important news.

"All right," Clint said. "The dessert is here. What's so important that you have to tell me?"

"It's big, Clint."

"I know! That's all you've said about it. Say something else before I get up and walk away."

Scott smiled, which wasn't exactly appealing on his round, bulbous face. A few years ago, he might have looked like an overgrown child. Now, he just looked like an overripe apple that had been peeled and covered in butter. Wiping some of the sweat that had accumulated on his brow, Scott said, "I'm considering opening a store."

"Yeah?"

"Yeah."

Clint blinked and waited until his patience ran out. "That's your big news?"

"Yes!"

Looking around as if he expected someone at another table to inform him of what he was missing, Clint said, "A store?"

"Yes! My own store."

"What kind of store?"

"A feed store," Scott proudly announced.

Leaning back in his chair, Clint placed both hands on the table and eyed Scott suspiciously. "You're full of shit."

"Nope."

"And why the hell is this such big news?"

"Because it's me, Clint. That's why. I'm the man who's spent most of his life either getting into fights, rolling out of the wrong woman's bed or cooling my heels in jail."

"Usually after doing one or both of the first two things you mentioned," Clint said.

Both of them laughed for a short while before Scott shifted his gaze downward at the cake in front of him.

"A good part of my life, I've felt like I didn't know what I was doing," he said quietly.

Matching Scott's tone, Clint said, "Kind of like when you ordered a whole cake instead of two pieces?"

Scott nodded.

"Maybe. I just felt like I wanted to celebrate and it didn't seem right celebrating the way I usually do."

"Usually, we have a beer to celebrate," Clint pointed out. "That's how most men do it."

"Right, but I ain't most men. I start drinking and I don't stop until I'm passed out on the floor, in a fight or in jail."

After a short bit of thinking, Clint nodded.

"I suppose that's true. Guess I never really thought it was something to be concerned about."

"When I'm around you, I try to be on my best behavior."

"You do?"

"Sure," Scott said. "You're a known man, and not for the bad reasons."

"Some folks may take issue with you on that."

"Them folks are assholes. Most of my life, I was one too. I always been content to be that way, too. But all that's changed. It's time I stop living at the bottom of a bottle and living like a damn dog."

"You want to be respectable?" Clint asked.

"Eh, let's not go that far."

Clint picked up the knife that Hallie had brought them and used it to carve out a piece of cake.

"What's her name?" he asked.

"Her who?"

"Usually when a man decides to make a big change like this, there's a her involved."

"Oh," Scott said with a little cringe. "There may be one, but she's not exactly why I'm doing this."

"Really?" Clint asked skeptically.

"Yes! Hell, I ain't even been alone with her yet. At least, not very long."

"But this mystery woman does have something to do with your line of thinking?"

Scott sighed and started cutting his own piece of cake. "Is it always so damn important for you to be right all the time?"

"I can't help it if that's just the way things usually work out," Clint said with overblown bravado. He kept it up for a few seconds before chuckling.

"It's nothing to be ashamed of," he said. "There are plenty worse reasons to do something. So, what's her name?"

After a bit of fidgeting in his seat, Scott replied, "Abigail. But she doesn't know anything about this and she surely doesn't know I look at her as anything other than a good friend."

"Well, that's gotta change," Clint declared. "Life's too short to muck around where love is concerned."

"She wouldn't have anything to do with a man like me. At least," Scott added, "not with the man I've been most of my life. She's a good woman. She's . . ."

As Scott searched for the right word to use, Clint offered, "Respectable?"

"Yes! She's respectable and she don't deserve anything less from a man who wants to be with her."

Clint nodded while taking a bite of cake.

"That's probably the kindest thing I've ever heard you say, Scott. Especially where women are concerned."

"Do me a favor, huh?"

"What?"

"If you ever do meet Abigail, don't bring up anything about any of the other women I been with."

Putting on the airs of a Georgia plantation owner, Clint said, "Why would I want to bring up such sordid subjects with a respectable woman?"

"Exactly. Thank you."

The two of them ate their cake for a few more moments in silence. There was a commotion building outside, but hadn't become big enough to garner Clint's full attention. Finally, Clint asked, "You're really giving up the old life and opening a feed store?"

"That's my plan."

"Why a feed store?"

"Because," Scott replied, "it was on sale by the previous owner and I managed to get a good deal on it. All I had to do was some repairs, and some extensions."

"Let me guess. You won it in a poker game?"

Scott tried to appear offended, but couldn't keep up the act for long. "Something like that," he grudgingly admitted.

Clint smirked. "It's good to see some things haven't changed."

The commotion outside had gained quite a bit of steam in the space of a few seconds. What had started as a few raised voices had grown into a gathering that was sizeable enough for Clint to see through the lacy curtains of the window across the room from his table.

"What's going on out there?" Scott asked through a mouthful of cake. "Somebody getting into a fight?"

"I don't know," Clint said. "Whatever it is, it seems serious."

"Eh, let 'em fight. Just so long as it doesn't make its way into this place, we'll be fine right where we are."

Clint pushed away from the table and stood up. Placing his napkin down, he narrowed his eyes to study the window while walking slowly across the room. As he neared the front of the restaurant, Clint's hand drifted toward the holster hanging at his side.

As Clint stepped outside, Scott stayed put and shook his head. "Yessiree," he sighed. "Some things ain't never gonna change."

Chapter Four

There was a good mix of people on the street outside the restaurant. They ranged from young to old, men and women, rich and poor. Every second that passed, more folks wandered in from other directions to make the group even larger. It wasn't the people themselves that put Clint on edge. There was a crackling in the air that he could feel in his bones.

A storm was brewing.

Judging by the frantic voices and pale faces around him, the storm was already there.

"What's going on here?" Clint asked the first person he could find.

The man was dressed in simple clothes and looked to be somewhere in his thirties. He stood on the edge of the boardwalk, which put him on the outer periphery of the crowd. He snapped his head back to look at Clint, but was just as quick to shift his attention to the commotion brewing in front of him.

"Someone got killed," the man said.

"Where," Clint asked while looking for the eye of the storm in front of him. "At one of the saloons?"

The restaurant was close enough to the ruckus to get a good look at it, but not so that Clint could hear what was being said while standing directly in front of it. The more he watched, the more the people started to mill about listlessly. They spilled from the street, onto the boardwalk and some even hurried away altogether.

"Wasn't no saloon fight," the younger man said. "Not what I heard. Someone cut apart a couple of old timers down by Farley's."

"Farley's?"

"It's not too far from here," the man replied while pointing to the eastern section of town.

Clint searched his memory of Alban to run through the names of the gambling parlors, opium dens or whorehouses in the area. With a place like Alban, such establishments came and went almost as quickly as the sailors working their way up and down the Mississippi. Farley's, however, didn't ring any bells for him.

"What happened to them?" Clint asked.

"I don't know. All I heard was that they got sliced up pretty good by an Injun or something along those lines."

"So they're not sure."

The younger man merely shrugged.

"Are the old timers still alive?" Clint asked.

The younger man pondered that for a second before saying, "I don't think so. I reckon there wouldn't be such a fuss if they were. Then again, there was a man who cut up a whore one time and that stirred up a whole mess. She's still alive."

Centering his eyes on a man standing in the street doing his best to address as many people as he could, Clint asked, "That's the town law?"

It took the other man a moment or two, but he eventually spotted the man in Clint's sights. "Yeah, that's Sheriff Tyson."

"You think he'll know what's going on?"

"If anyone does, it'd be him."

Clint stepped down from the boardwalk and made his way to the center of the crowd. Almost immediately, he was shoved, jostled and knocked around by the sea of flailing arms and stumbling bodies. On every side, people were gesturing wildly or trying to get close enough to hear what was being said by the town's lawman. Since he was headed in that same direction, Clint had to get a little forceful to make sure he made any progress at all.

"Everyone needs to back the hell up and calm the hell down!" the sheriff hollered, which didn't do much to calm the people around him.

Several men fought to get the sheriff's attention by tapping him on the shoulder or even grabbing hold of his arm to pull him in one direction or another. The women in the group weren't much better, since they asserted themselves by raising their voices more and more to be heard over the rest.

"Where are the Marshalls?" someone asked.

"Who attacked them?"

"I heard it was Indians!" a woman announced.

To that, a gravelly voiced man in the crowd hollered, "Find the damned redskins and string 'em up!"

"I heard it was just one man that did it."

"I heard it was a gang of 'em."

The voices came from everywhere at once. Before long, it was almost impossible to tell where each voice was coming from. The sheriff attempted to sort through it and provide some answers where he could, but his words were swallowed up by the churning mass of excited paranoia.

Sheriff Tyson tried to get some space by moving an older man back. When that man bumped into another man, they started grousing at each other. The sheriff tried to stop that, which only added more fuel to the fire.

A few seconds later, a single gunshot exploded through the air to stop everyone in their tracks.

The entire crowd jumped away from the source of the shot. After that, everyone turned to look in that direction while the sheriff and a few others drew their own weapons.

Clint stood on a small patch of ground that had just been cleared. His smoking Colt was still in hand, which he eased back down into its holster. He hated drawing his gun when he didn't have to, but this situation seemed to call for it.

"Now that I have everyone's attention," he said, "let's try to go about this in a more civilized manner."

Chapter Five

"And who the hell are you?" the lawman asked.

Keeping his voice as calm as possible, Clint replied, "My name's Clint Adams. What's going on out here?"

Although he bristled at being questioned by a stranger, the sheriff said, "Seems like that's what everyone here wants to know."

"Damn right it is," shouted someone in the crowd. Before that sentiment could be repeated and built up again, the sheriff started talking in a loud, commanding tone.

"There's been a killing. One of the Hoover boys found the bodies a few minutes ago."

"Who was killed?" Clint asked.

"Old couple who's lived here a good number of years. Miles and Kate Marshall."

A ripple of emotion worked its way through the people gathered in the street. Unlike the last wave of emotion that had surrounded those same people, this time there was more shock and despair to be felt rather than anger and confusion. Some of the women in the vicinity turned away and walked from the street, their shoulders trembling with heartfelt sobs.

Stepping closer to the lawman so he didn't have to talk so loudly to be heard, Clint asked, "How were they killed?"

"They were cut up pretty bad."

"Where are they now?"

"One of my deputies is with them, as well as the doctor. I was on my way there when this mob decided to form and keep me from doing my job."

When he said that last part, the sheriff turned to look at as many of the people in the street as he could. Some of them returned his gaze while others shifted uneasily where they stood.

"I'm going to get a better look for myself," Tyson continued. "Any of you folks follow me to try and get a gander at what's left of them poor people, you'll be spending the night in a jail cell. Am I clear?"

There were a few grunts in the crowd as some of its members drifted away.

Looking at the more stubborn remaining locals, the sheriff growled, "I said, am I clear?"

None of the holdouts kept their resolve and they decided to find somewhere else to be.

When the sheriff started walking away, he quickly realized he wasn't alone. "I thought I made myself clear," he said without looking at the man falling into step beside him.

"You certainly did," Clint said as he matched the lawman's pace.

"Then why are you still here?"

"Thought I'd lend a hand."

"With what? You some kind of doctor?"

"No."

"How about a butcher, then?" the lawman asked in a tired voice. "From what little I saw of it, that sounds more like the sort of man I'll need to make sense of this."

"I've seen a lot of dead men," Clint said. "More than I'd like, but it does give me something of an eye for this sort of thing."

"Have you ever tracked a killer?"

"Yes, I have."

The sheriff glanced over at Clint and nodded once.

"Yeah, I thought you looked like that sort of fella. The way you stepped in and got that crowd to quiet down made me think you've had some experience as a peace officer."

"All I did was fire a gun at the sky."

The sheriff approached Clint with his thumbs hooked over his belt and his eyes narrowed in intense concentration. When he examined Clint, he did it carefully and methodically. Once he was finished, Tyson shook his head and grinned.

"You've worn a badge before. I'd stake my life on it. That kind of thing shows on a man just as plainly as the shirt on his back. At least, it does when you know what to look for."

"I may have served on a few posses," Clint admitted.

The sheriff shrugged as if to concede the point, even though he suspected there was a lot more to be said on the matter. "You've tracked outlaws, I reckon."

"I have."

"Then come along with me," the lawman said, turning his back on Clint and walking away as though he knew he would be followed. After a few more steps, Tyson glanced over to see that Clint was indeed walking beside him.

"Where have you ridden in a posse?" Tyson asked.

"New Mexico, Texas, some in the Dakota Territories."

"That all?"

"No."

"What's your name, anyway?"

"Clint Adams."

The lawman stopped and turned to face Clint head-on. "Clint Adams?"

"That's what I said."

"I've heard of you from a couple of peace officers from West Texas."

"Mostly good, I hope," Clint said.

"Yeah, mostly. Are you squeamish?"

"Not particularly."

"That might change once you see what was left in this alley I'm taking you to."

Chapter Six

The alley was wide enough to accommodate two horses walking side by side all the way down. There were several buildings that formed the space, all of which were either locked up for the night or boarded up completely. As soon as Clint was close enough to see the cart that was parked in that alley, he could smell the blood that had been spilled there.

Two men stood at the mouth of the alley. One was a younger fellow with fair hair and wide shoulders. He shifted nervously on his feet, keeping his hands close to the holster at his side without any target to shoot.

The other man was older and had a stooped posture. His skin was pasty, and he smoked a cigar with all the easiness of a gentleman on his porch after a filling meal.

"Where'd everyone go?" the sheriff asked as he approached the younger of the two near the alley.

"Sent 'em home," the young man replied. When he spotted Clint, he puffed his chest out and placed his hands on his hips to display the gun, and deputy's badge he wore. "Who's this?"

"It's all right," Tyson replied. "I brought him along." To Clint, he said, "There were a whole gaggle of folks crowded around here when the bodies were found. Morbid curiosity and all that."

"Let's get a look for ourselves, then," Clint said. He did his best to ignore the stench of death that only grew more pungent as he was led into the alley. That smell wasn't unfamiliar to him, but he would never get used to it. The day he did become accustomed to such a thing would be the day he hung up his gun for good.

At first, all Clint could see were shadows in the alley. After taking a few more steps, he could make out a pair of bodies lying on the ground. They were propped up, sitting side by side with their backs to the same wall. Their arms were splayed out to their sides and their heads lolled forward upon slit throats.

Blood seeped down from their necks, soaking into their clothes. Their legs were situated neatly in front of them. What drew Clint's attention the most was the fact that both of the elderly victims had had their bellies cut open to put all of their innards on display. The flaps of their skin were pulled apart, allowing entrails to slide out of place and spill down in a gruesome cascade.

"Jesus H Christ," Tyson whispered.

"Yeah," Clint replied solemnly. "But I don't think he was anywhere around this place tonight."

"Who would do this sort of thing?"

Squatting down to get a closer look at the old man, Clint asked, "Do you know these two?"

"Miles and Kate Marshall. They've lived here since long before I was sheriff in this town."

"Did they have any enemies?"

"Enemies?" the deputy barked. "Miles went to church every Sunday! He helped build my house! Kate would mend clothes for anyone who needed it without asking for a cent! What kind of damned question is that?"

"Just a question," Clint said. "Asking them is the best way to figure this out."

"He's right, Bill," the sheriff said as he placed a hand on the younger man's shoulder. "Why don't you go back to where you were?"

"You mean with Grinsby?" the deputy asked distastefully.

"That's right. Keep him and anyone else who might come along from wandering in here."

Giving Clint one more glare, the deputy grunted, "Fine," before walking away.

"All right, then," Tyson said. "Let's get to work."

"Who's that other man out there?" Clint asked.

"Undertaker. Mark Grinsby."

Clint nodded while gently touching the edge of the gaping wound in the old man's belly. "Whoever did this wasn't out to rob these folks, that's for certain. Also wasn't just some angry drunk or upset family member."

"What about an Injun? Some folks said it could've been done by one or even a small pack of redskins."

Clint shook his head. "This doesn't go along with anything I've ever seen in regard to any of the tribes. Of course, the killer may or may not be an Indian, just as he may or may not be Mexican or white. That's just not important here."

"What is important?"

"That he's not in his right mind."

The sheriff laughed uneasily. "Hell, I could've told you just by looking at this here that whoever did this is some kind of raving loon."

"Not raving," Clint said, shaking his head. "These bodies were placed here and killed in the same way. Some wild man would have just ripped them up with no regard to propping them up or putting on a show like this."

"Show?" The sheriff sneered. All he had to do was look at the scene and the way the old couple was presenting themselves to admit, "I guess I see your point there. For all we know, this could've been done by a woman."

"Not likely. Whoever did this had to be strong. Maybe intimidating. These wounds are smooth. There was barely any struggle."

"The killer was either very strong or real quick," Tyson pointed out.

"Strong, quick or both," Clint said. "Whichever it is, they're still out there."

Chapter Seven

Clint took a careful look around at the alley while keeping his eyes open for anything else that might be important. He spotted one thing that struck him as peculiar, but didn't mention it to the sheriff. Instead, he finished his search of the alley and its grounds before stepping back so the undertaker could do his work.

From what little he'd heard about the Marshalls, they were good people. Good people didn't deserve to die that way and they sure as hell didn't deserve to stay out in the open with their guts spread out for all to see. After a short bit of preparation, the undertaker bundled both bodies up so they could be loaded onto the back of a wagon which he brought around straight away.

Clint agreed to meet the sheriff the following day when they had some sunlight to work by. Until then, the lawmen were more than happy to get away from that hellish alley and turn their efforts back to the curious locals that insisted on pestering them as they headed back to their office.

After walking down one street in the direction of the hotel where he was renting a room, Clint turned a corner and headed for a stretch of road that was lined mostly with houses and small shacks. Those structures were dark at that time of night, allowing him to circle back around to the alley where the killings had happened without being seen. Just to be certain, however, he kept his steps light and was careful to check behind him and on all sides.

Nobody was trailing behind him.

There was no one on the street.

None of the windows were opened.

When he arrived at the street with the blood stained alley, Clint was as certain as he could be that he was alone.

Whoever had gutted those two old folks must have known the law would be after them. The murderer had either already left town or was trying to keep from being caught while laying low right there in Alban. If the former was the case, then Clint knew he wouldn't be able to catch up with them that night anyway after the large head start the killer had already gotten. If the latter was true, he didn't want to risk being spotted by anyone trying to keep watch on whoever might be trying to hunt them down.

Once he was there, Clint realized he'd stopped just short of entering the alley. He hadn't thought about keeping still, but his feet simply didn't want to carry him any further. The thoughts of what had been there not so long ago were still as fresh as the vile odor that clung to the back of his throat. The scent of blood was still in the air, almost like the cloud of stink that hung above a slaughterhouse.

Shaking his head, Clint forced himself to carry on. He hadn't met the Marshalls before that night. He'd seen blood before. He'd witnessed more than his share of death. Somehow, no matter how much he told himself those things, he couldn't enter that alley without feeling a knot in the pit of his stomach.

This time, his eyes were no longer forced to take in the sight of those two poor souls lying on the ground. He could look at the ground and the surrounding area for anything that might give him a hint as to who'd wielded that blade and where they might have gone once the Marshalls were dead.

Seeing that place in the darkness wasn't as much a hindrance as most people might have thought. Although he couldn't make out small details, Clint could see the alley laid out in a simpler fashion. Shapes and forms showed themselves without being marred by color and movement. The first thing he noticed under those stark circumstances was the placement of the wagon that had been parked in that alley.

The wagon was no longer there, but it was easy enough to tell where it had been. Clint's memory, combined with the ruts in the ground and the tracks left behind by the horses were more than enough for him to recall the cart's exact position. The strange thing was that it was several feet away from where it should have been.

There was a hitching rail near the back of the alley. There were also some crates that were stacked along one of the walls on the same side where the wagon had been as well as another awkwardly stacked pile against the opposite wall. When Clint got a bit closer, he could see deep imprints in the ground of where one stack had been piled directly in front of the crates where the wagon had been parked. He picked up one crate to be certain and sure enough, it fit perfectly within the imprint on the ground.

Apparently, all of the crates had been stacked together not so long ago. In fact, looking at the alley as a simple collection of shapes and angles, it made more sense for them all to be arranged in one spot since that would keep the crates from blocking any of the doors leading into the buildings that formed the alley.

Clint stepped back and looked at the less organized of the two stacks. In the quiet night and inky shadows, the stack looked like the one thing in that alley that didn't belong. Even though the rest of the alley was far from straight edges and perfect angles, those crates stuck out like a busted nose.

Someone must have moved those crates to form two piles. Judging by the look of one of those piles, whoever had moved them had done so in a hurry. If they were in a hurry, they were probably trying to get something done that needed doing in private.

As Clint stood there fitting the pieces together in his mind, he wasn't quite getting to the answer. He stepped into the alley and stood in roughly the same spot he'd been when he'd first gotten a glimpse at the bodies of Miles and Kate Marshall.

At the mouth of the alley, he could look down all the way to the end. If he was going to spring an ambush in that spot, the main concern would be being spotted. There wasn't much cover in the alley. At least, not at the moment. Clint narrowed his eyes and imagined where the wagon had been and immediately realized it had blocked almost the entire line of sight from the back end of the alley.

In fact, considering the spot where most of the blood had dried on the wall, the spot where the murders had occurred was mostly blocked by the wagon from the front end of the alley as well. If the wagon had been closer to the hitching rail, the entire alley would have been considerably more organized and easier to navigate. Having the wagon moved just that little bit, along with those crates, created a jagged little piece of enclosed space that would have been tough to spot from the street. With the sun already down, the killer would have had a good amount of privacy.

As Clint took all of that in, he heard soft footsteps approaching. They came from the street and when he turned to see who it was, he expected to find one of the town's lawmen there to ask him what he thought he was doing. Instead, he saw a slender man bundled in a black wool coat.

"Chilly night," the man said.

"Yeah," Clint replied.

"You hear about what happened in that alley?"

"I did. Terrible. Really terrible."

"Sure is," the man said as he stepped closer and pulled a knife from his coat pocket.

Chapter Eight

Clint barely saw the knife until it was too late. The slender man moved so fluidly that he barely seemed like a threat before taking a quick, lunging swing at him. Clint twisted to one side, reacting more from the proximity of the other man's arm instead of anything the slender fellow was doing. That instinct allowed him to dodge most of the blade apart from a little piece of its sharpened edge. The knife sliced through Clint's shirt like butter, sending drops of blood to the dirt.

Raising his arms and hopping back, Clint pivoted around to face the man in front of him. The man still had one hand stuffed into the pocket of his coat and lashed out with his right to take another stab at Clint. Unlike many attackers, his moves weren't wild or desperate. The instant his blade was past its target, he snapped that hand back to flick it out again. The knife was almost an extension of his hand and was sharp enough to do most of the work where killing was concerned.

Clint attempted to reach for his Colt, but he wasn't fast enough to get to his holster before the blade was slicing through the air toward him yet again. If that wasn't a big enough feat, the slender man was able to change the direction of his swing quickly enough to angle the blade inward and rake it along Clint's forearm. This was possibly the best knife fighter Clint had ever seen.

Taking a few shuffling steps back, Clint tried to catch his breath. He got less than half an inhale before the slender man lunged at him. In the time it took to blink in surprise, Clint had to raise both arms to protect his face before it was cut from his skull. Fortunately, his block managed to stop the slender man's arm before it could get the blade close enough to do any damage. Locked with their arms pushing against one another, Clint stared straight into the eyes of his attacker.

The slender man looked back at him with a glimmer in his eye that could have been mistaken for mischievous glee. There wasn't a hint of rage or murderous intent in there. Nothing at all matched the face of a man who was fighting for his life or for the moment to take the life of someone else. As Clint looked at him, the slender man simply looked back.

Having seen more than enough, Clint lifted one leg to drive his knee into the slender man's gut. When he grunted at the impact, the slender man let out what sounded like half a laugh. Clint tried once again to draw his Colt, but was stopped by the quick slash of his opponent. Feinting as though he meant to draw with his other hand across his body, Clint got the slender man to swing again. This time, he used some quickness of his own to grab hold of the other man's wrist.

"What are you doing out here?" Clint asked as he struggled to keep the knife from being reclaimed by its owner.

The slender man put up a hell of a fight, nearly pulling free of Clint's grip several times before he said, "Just a nice night for a stroll."

"You killed those old folks, didn't you?"

The slender man grinned.

"Why would you do that?" Clint asked. "Was it a robbery? Do you know those two?"

But the slender man wasn't about to be distracted by small talk. He kicked Clint's shin with the pointed toe of his boot and then kicked him again. When that didn't get Clint to relent, he dug his bony fingertips into Clint's face. If Clint hadn't pulled away when he did, he would've been missing an eye. As it was, he came away with a few bloody scrapes in his cheek.

Thinking he'd bought himself some room, Clint slapped his hand against his holster with the intent of drawing the Colt. He cleared leather, but not before the slender man threw himself at him. Anyone with a lick of sense would have been cautious when attacking someone who had a pistol in his hand. This man, however, showed no concern for the Colt. Even when the pistol barked twice in short order, the slender man sidestepped around Clint until he could reach around his neck from behind.

As Clint felt those two skinny arms snake around his throat, he angled his gun up and back to aim over his shoulder. The barrel was pointed straight up when Clint heard a grating voice in his ear.

"Ah, ah," the slender man whispered. "If you shoot now, it might make me twitch." When he said that last word, he wiggled one hand against the side of Clint's throat.

Feeling the knife's blade scrape against his jugular, Clint froze where he stood. "If you're just gonna kill me, I might as well kill you," Clint said.

"You could try."

Clint thought about making his move and the blade pressed a little harder against his skin.

"So, what now?" he asked while trying to move as little as possible.

"I don't know. That's the beauty of it."

"You killed those two old folks."

"Oh, yes."

"Why?"

"What kind of a question is that?" the slender man hissed, showing the first hint of emotion thus far.

Knowing he wasn't going to get a better opening, Clint took hold of the slender man's arm and pulled it away from his neck. He couldn't get it far, but he managed to make enough space to wriggle free and spin around. By the time he was facing the right direction, Clint no longer had such an easy target.

The slender man had already taken off running in the opposite direction, his coat tails flapping behind him.

Clint fired at the slender man once, but didn't stop him. He fired again, just as the slender man turned sharply to race along the side of the street. Holding his pistol in front of him, Clint fixed his eyes on the slender man's back. Rather than shoot a fleeing man, he set his sights a little lower and fired again.

The slender man wasn't much more than a shadowy outline when he staggered for a few steps and veered toward a row of darkened buildings. Clint continued to run after him, his hands going through the practiced motions of reloading the Colt as his legs carried him onward.

After a few more steps, Clint saw another alley. That was the spot where the slender man must have gone since he was nowhere to be found on the street or on the boardwalk. Clint stopped short of charging into a possible ambush so he could try and get a glimpse of what might be waiting for him down that alley.

Clint heard hurried footsteps, but they came from the other end of the alley. He almost ran into the shadows after them, but stopped short when he thought of all the different ways the slender man could jump him from there. Launching into a dead run, Clint circled around that building to reach the back end of the alley.

There was nobody waiting for him there and no more footsteps to be heard. Whoever was there before was gone now. A careful check of the alley confirmed as much.

"God dammit," Clint snarled under his breath.

Chapter Nine

Clint was still muttering angrily under his breath as he walked past the Tres Bouchet. The restaurant was closing by that time and a few stragglers were walking out through the front door. Without lifting his head to get a look at any of them, Clint kept right on walking down the boardwalk. All he looked for was another attack. If no attack was coming, he just wanted to keep moving.

"Clint?"

He didn't stop when he heard his name. In fact, Clint tried to act as though he hadn't even heard the familiar voice.

Hurried footsteps sounded behind him as the person who'd spoken his name rushed to catch up to him. Soon, Clint felt a gentle hand touch his shoulder.

"Clint? Are you bleeding?"

Clint stopped and straightened his posture. His hand was kept close to his side to keep the bloody portion of his forearm out of sight. Judging by the worried expression on Hallie's face, he wasn't doing a very good job.

"Yeah," he said. "A little."

The server looked him up and down, placing her hands on him here and there as though she was afraid she might break him. "What happened?"

"Nothing, really. Thanks for asking, though." With that, he turned to walk away.

She kept pace with him, wrapping one arm around him and gingerly touching his bloody arm.

"You're hurt. Tell me what happened? Were you attacked by those Indians?"

"There are no Indians in town," Clint snapped. "At least, none that should be of concern to anyone."

"But you were attacked."

"Yes. Now I'd like to clean up and get some sleep if that's all right with you."

Almost immediately, Clint regretted the way he'd barked at her. Hallie was never anything but kind and warm to him. The fact that she'd stopped to ask about the blood on his clothes while everyone else was content to let him pass them by said plenty about her character.

A few seconds after she pulled away from him, Clint stopped and turned around to look at her directly.

"Sorry about that," he said. "I shouldn't have spoken to you that way."

"It's all right," she replied meekly.

"No. It isn't. I really am tired."

"And hurt," she added.

"Yeah. That also, but not too badly."

Both of them started walking again, side by side. Although she didn't wrap her arm around him, Hallie stayed close to Clint as she asked, "How many men attacked you?"

"Just one. He was a wild one, though."

"I bet he was." After a few seconds, she asked, "Was he the one who killed the Marshalls?"

"Yeah. He was."

"Did you . . .?"

"No," Clint said before she could get the rest of her question out. "I didn't kill him. Next time I see him, though, things will go a lot differently."

"Next time?"

"A bastard like that can't be allowed to roam free," he said. "It'll only be a matter of time before he kills again."

"Maybe he just had it out for Miles Marshall. Or Kate, although I'd find that hard to believe."

"So what if he did?" Clint asked. "You think he should be treated any better?"

"Not at all! I'm just saying if he meant to kill one or both of them, he already did it. If that's the case, then he doesn't have any reason to kill again." She blinked nervously and wiped at her eyes with the back of one hand. "Then he can just go away and not come back."

Suddenly, Clint felt like an absolute ass. Hallie wasn't trying to justify anything that happened or speak on anyone's behalf. She was scared, plain and simple. She was frightened about a bloodthirsty killer roaming the streets of her town and didn't want to think about meeting that killer herself.

Clint lowered his head a bit. When she tried to look away, he gently moved her chin so she looked at him again.

"That killer has had enough for one night. I saw to that personally. He may not be dead, but he's not going to bother anyone for a while. Understand?"

Hallie nodded.

"Did you know the Marshalls?"

"Not very well," she replied. "I served them dinner every other Sunday and breakfast three times a week. They were quiet, at least to me. But they were nice folks."

"I didn't know them at all," Clint admitted, "but I still don't want their killer to get away with what he's done."

Hallie nodded again, this time with more resolve.

"It's been a long night," he continued.

"And you're still hurt," she quickly said. "You're cut pretty bad. You need to be stitched up."

"Maybe I should see the doctor."

"No," she said as she wrapped an arm around him and steered him down the street. "You're coming with me."

Chapter Ten

Clint sat on the edge of a soft bed on a sturdy wooden frame. He was in a room that was sparsely furnished, yet very comfortable and warm. The only light came from a lantern setting on a nearby table and a fireplace built into the wall. It was one of two rooms in Hallie's cabin, situated near the edge of town.

His shirt was off and his arm was still damp from being washed. "Where did you learn to do such good work?" he asked while admiring the new stitches that had been put into his wounded forearm.

Hallie shrugged. "This isn't the first rough place I've lived. I must've picked it up along the way."

"Well I appreciate the help. You're a lot more comforting than any doctor."

She smiled, put down the wet rag she'd been holding and sat down on the bed next to him. At first, she merely smiled at him. Then, she reached out to place a hand on his cheek to hold him in place as she leaned over to kiss him on the lips. The move seemed to surprise both of them. It didn't take long for Clint to make his move and he kissed her right back.

Hallie's lips parted as Clint started to move away, her tongue flicking out to taste his lips one last time before the kiss was through.

"I've been wanting to do that for a while," he said.

"Me too," she whispered.

Clint took her in his arms and eased her onto the bed. Hallie laid down and started kissing him intently, wrapping her arms around him while digging her nails into his back with growing passion. When his hands found their way to her breasts, she let out a shuddering moan and arched her back.

He removed her blouse and skirts in a rush, getting her out of her clothes completely thanks to some help from Hallie's eager hands. When she was naked, Hallie started tugging at Clint's belt so she could reach inside his pants to feel his growing erection.

Clint set his gunbelt on the floor within easy reach, and kicked out of his jeans. As he settled between Hallie's legs, she tugged anxiously at the buttons of his shirt so she could rub her hands flat against his chest. Her body was smooth and soft to the touch. Her wide hips filled his hands as Clint explored every inch of her. When he moved his fingers to her inner thighs, Hallie moaned softly and spread her legs even wider.

Clint rubbed her pussy until it was wet and ready for him. Then, with a guiding hand from Hallie herself, he eased his cock between the slick lips of her pussy. As Clint entered her, Hallie wrapped her legs around him. When Clint had slipped every inch of his rigid penis inside of her, Hallie bit her lower lip and tightened her grip on him to keep Clint from moving a muscle.

For a few moments, Clint stayed still. He drank in the sight of her bare breasts and savored the feel of her skin as he moved his hands up and down the length of her body. Then he started pumping in and out of her, slowly at first but building quickly into a steady rhythm.

He rode her for a while, sliding between her thighs as she grunted with pleasure every time their bodies met. Clint took hold of her hands, pinning Hallie's arms against the mattress on either side of her head. She smiled up at him and gasped as his rigid cock filled her one more time. As he eased out of her, Hallie glanced over to Clint's stitched arm.

"Oh no," she said.

"What? What is it?"

"Your arm. This must be hurting your arm."

"Forget about that," Clint said as he shifted once more between her legs. But Hallie wasn't going to let him get very far before she started wriggling out from underneath him.

"What are you doing?" he asked. "I'm fine."

"You let me be the judge of that," she said as she rolled Clint onto his back so she could climb on top of him. Once she'd mounted him, she reached down and guided his rigid penis between her thighs. "Yes," she sighed as he slipped into her. "You're fine now."

Hallie sat upright as she began rocking on top of him. Taking Clint deep inside of her, she reached up with both hands to slide her fingers through her hair.

Clint's hands went straight to her firm breasts, massaging them and cupping them as she rode his cock. Her nipples became hard right away and when he found the best spot, she clamped her hands on top of his to keep them from moving away. She started bouncing on top of him faster, grinding him against the place inside of her that brought her to a shuddering climax.

Sweat broke out on her brow, trickling all the way down her neck to form tiny rivulets between her breasts. Once her orgasm subsided, she lowered herself down so her face was close enough to kiss Clint on the mouth.

Clint moved his hands along her body, down her back until they came to a rest on her nicely rounded buttocks. Gazing up at her, Clint rubbed the sides of her hips before giving her a playful slap with both hands. Hallie's eyes widened and she drew a quick breath.

"You like that?" Clint asked.

"Maybe."

He rubbed her again, gave her a softer slap on the hips and then drove his cock up into her. She grunted and held her face within a few inches of Clint's.

"I like that," she told him. "A lot."

Clint smiled and pumped into her a few times. His hands moved around to cup her ass. That way, he could pull her close as he drove his cock between her thighs. Keeping his grip there, he held her in place as he pumped faster and harder.

Hallie's mouth was so close to Clint's ear that he could hear every excited breath as he thrust into her. She made contented little sounds as she was brought closer and closer to another climax. When he tightened his grip on her backside, Clint pumped into her with strong, powerful strokes. Her body began to tremble and she groaned with pleasure.

Every muscle in Clint's body strained with the effort of driving his cock into her again and again. His pace became feverish as he drew closer to the height of his pleasure. Hallie gripped him tightly, breathing in fast, shallow gasps. After a few more strokes, Clint exploded inside of her.

When he opened his eyes again, she was looking down at him. Her hair was tussled and her cheeks flushed. Setting her chin down onto his chest, she looked into his eyes and asked, "Feeling better?"

"Yeah," Clint chuckled. "You got one hell of a bedside manner."

Chapter Eleven

The following morning, Clint woke up alone in Hallie's bed. He recalled her waking up some time earlier, but it was well before sunrise and they'd worn each other out the night before. She'd told him something about her needing to go back to the restaurant to help make breakfast, but that he could stay as long as he wanted and let himself out. After a bit more sleep, he'd done just that.

When he walked back to the Tres Bouchet, Clint found Scott at the same table he'd been at the previous day. Pulling up a chair to sit across from the other man, Clint asked, "Do you ever leave this place?"

"Not when they're serving flapjacks!" Scott replied. "Have some."

"Don't mind if I do."

Although Hallie wasn't the one serving them, she smiled at Clint from the kitchen as she helped mix up another batch of batter.

Scott poured some coffee from the pot on his table into the cup that had been set there for the next customer.

"So," he said while waggling his eyebrows, "you seem pretty chipper this morning."

"I do?"

"Why do you sound so surprised? Didn't you and Hallie spend some time together last night?"

"How do you know about that?" Clint asked.

"Small town," Scott replied. "Also," he added while waving a hand around to encompass the entire place, "there's plenty of women working here and they all like to talk."

Considering the early hour and lack of card games being played at any of the tables, talking was the main thing going on apart from eating in the Tres Bouchet. When Clint looked around at the other servers, he got more than a few glances in return from the other waitresses.

"I would think folks would have something else to talk about," Clint grumbled before taking a sip of coffee.

"Like what?" Scott asked.

"Are you joking? There was a murder not too far from here last night."

"Oh, that."

"Yeah," Clint said. "That. How could anyone forget?"

"This is a port town," Scott said. "Lots of sailors. Lots of merchants. Lots of thieves and outlaws. That means lots of blood spilled on a daily basis."

"Maybe, but not like this."

Scott leaned forward and dropped his voice to a whisper. "Really? You're talking about the Marshalls, right?"

"Yeah."

"How bad was it?"

The memories washed over Clint like a waking nightmare, which he immediately tried to force into the back of his head where they'd been. To Scott, he said, "Real bad."

"I heard it was Indians that did it."

"Wasn't Indians."

"How can you be sure?"

Clint almost started explaining how it was he could be so sure. He almost started telling Scott about all of the trouble that had happened the night before. Before he got into that story, however, Clint noticed the brightness in Scott's eyes and the lightness of his manner. While he knew about the murders, they were just a juicy bit of gossip to him. The blood was barely real in Scott's mind and there was so much more to think about.

"Mostly a hunch, I guess," Clint said. "What's got you so cheery today?"

"I'm glad you asked! I'll be opening my store soon."

"Is that a fact?"

"It is," Scott replied. "It's taken a lot less time than I thought. Once I had most of the money pulled together, all I needed to do was rent the building and contact some suppliers. As it turns out, the building was pretty cheap and the suppliers were even more desperate for business than I am."

Clint chuckled. "So that means they're willing to make deliveries before getting a full payment."

"Exactly! I've known these men for a while, so they know they'll get their money. The sooner I open, the quicker I can start making profits."

"Tell me something. How'd you get your hands on all that money so quickly?"

"No need to worry about me, Clint. I've got it handled."

"See, now that's exactly the sort of thing that makes me worry."

Scott tried to keep a calm, excited expression on his face but it could only last so long. While there was definite excitement and enthusiasm in his eyes, there was also a slight hint of worry that seemed to go beyond that of the aspiring business-man.

"You never told me about the money," Clint reminded him. "I mean, apart from the fact that you had it."

"Is it so surprising that I might have saved up some money?"

"Yes."

Although Scott looked offended, he couldn't keep up the indignant expression for long. Eventually, he lowered his eyes and shrugged. "I may have had some problems with money in the past, but that's over now."

"Is it?" Clint asked.

"I just said so, didn't I?"

"You did, but is it really over?"

Scott looked up again and locked eyes with Clint. "Yes, it is. Mostly."

"There it is."

"There's what?"

"There's the hook," Clint said. "I don't mean to pry and I don't mean to kick sand on your fire, but there's always a hook with you. Especially where money is concerned."

"I thought you'd just be happy for me," Scott sighed.

"I am," Clint said. "I just also know how much trouble a man can get himself into where money is concerned. The more money that's involved, the bigger the trouble can be."

"And why did you decide to start raking me over the coals about it now?"

"I've been meaning to ask," Clint said. "Frankly, I was going to ask about it last night when you were in a happy frame of mind."

"You mean when I was drunk."

"That's not what I said," Clint replied defensively.

"You didn't have to say it, my friend. You claim to know me well, but I know you pretty good myself. You can be a real sneaky cuss when you want to be."

Wincing slightly, Clint said, "I'd prefer to think of it as strategic."

Grudgingly, Scott had to laugh.

"Sometimes it's better to do business with strangers, huh? They don't ask as many questions. Leastways, not as many of the questions that cut all the way down to the bone."

"So you borrowed some of that money you used to start your feed store," Clint said.

"That's right."

"And you borrowed it from men who don't exactly work for a bank."

Scott began to slowly shake his head.

"I really hate that you think so little of me. What I hate even more is that you're right."

"And these men," Clint continued. "Are they rough European types with scars on their faces and long mustaches?"

Scott's eyes widened.

"How the hell could you know that much?"

"Simple," Clint replied. "They just came in through the back and have been eyeing you the way a hungry dog looks at a pile of raw meat."

Chapter Twelve

Scott looked around slowly. Eventually, his gaze went to the table closest to the kitchen where two men were sitting. One of them had a thick build, a bushy mustache and scars that were deep and plentiful enough to be spotted from a distance. The other man at that table had a longer mustache that partly concealed his mouth and a scraggly beard.

"How long have they been there?" Scott asked.

"Not too long," Clint replied, "but they've been watching you like a hawk."

"Yeah. I didn't see them come in and I was watching the door the whole time."

"They didn't come in through that door," Clint said while nodding toward the front portion of the place. "They stepped in through that side door leading to the alley. It's the one used by the waitresses to come and go."

"You always did scout a place," Scott mused. "Even if it was just somewhere you meant to have a meal."

"It's a good habit to have, Scott. If you intend on doing business with the likes of them two, you might want to start learning that habit yourself."

"Now's not the time to rub my nose in it, Clint."

"All right. Who are they?"

Shifting nervously in his seat, Scott replied, "The one with the scars is Dane Miller. The other one is Bill Morrison. Or maybe it's Bob. I don't really know which."

"You three aren't on a first name basis?" Clint mused.

Sneering at the grin on Clint's face, Scott said, "I'm glad one of us thinks this is funny."

"Sorry. It's just nice to be the one who's not in someone's gun sights for a change."

"Shit, they're holding guns?"

"No," Clint snapped. "And lower your voice before you start a stampede in here."

The rest of the Tres Bouchet was filled with people eating and drinking. Some of them had started taking notice of what was happening at Clint's table and a few of them were starting to look more than a little nervous. It wasn't as bad as a stampede, but Clint didn't want to take any chances in such a crowded spot.

Whether he saw that point of view or not, Scott reined himself in a bit. "Have they seen me yet?" he asked.

"Are you joking?"

Scott let out a frustrated sigh. "I wish you would've told me as soon as they came in."

"And I wish you would've told me you had a couple of ugly bastards out looking to scalp you."

"They don't want to scalp me. At least, not yet. Besides, I didn't want to hear a sermon from you about how I shouldn't deal with outlaws or break the law or any of that kind of high and mighty stuff."

"You never change," Clint said. "How do you know those two anyway?"

"I was trying to pull some money together. And, before you ask, I did go to a bank first."

"Did you have a gun in your hand and a bandanna wrapped around your face at the time?" Clint asked.

"Very funny, asshole. No, I did not. I thought I'd try and do things the right way for a change and was turned down flat. Some stuck-up son of a bitch in a suit thought I should already own property to back up a loan they would give me to buy property! A friend of mine steered me toward some fellas who were in the business of loaning money to them that needs it."

"Come on, Scott," Clint scolded. "You should know better than to deal with men like that."

"I know I should know better, but sometimes a man's just gotta do what he can to make something happen, right?"

"Whatever you say," Clint grunted as he pushed his chair back and stood up.

"What are you doing?" Scott asked nervously.

"Going over there."

"Why?"

"To have a talk with them," Clint replied.

"They're not the talkative kind of men," Scott warned.

"Then it'll be a short conversation."

Chapter Thirteen

Clint could feel the glares being pointed at him from that table the instant he started walking across the room. Those two men stared at him with the intensity of sunlight being focused through a looking glass. Ignoring that as well as the scowls on their faces, Clint approached the table and sat down.

"Hello," he said.

"What the fuck you want?" the man with the bushy mustache asked.

"You're Dane, right?" Clint asked.

"What's it to you?"

"My name's Clint. I'm a friend of Scott Meyer over there."

Through the greasy whiskers of his drooping mustache, the other man said, "You should pick better friends."

"You may have a point there," Clint admitted. "But I thought I'd come over here to see what I could do on behalf of that particular friend anyhow. After that, perhaps I'll look into associating with a better class of people."

"You talk like a school marm," Dane said.

Deciding not to take offense at that, Clint asked, "How much does he owe you?"

"You mean your friend, Meyer?"

"That's right. How much?"

"Three thousand."

"That's a lot of money," Clint said.

"Damn right it is."

"It's a lot, but not too much for me to pull together on his behalf."

Dane's eyes narrowed into slits. "You're gonna pay off what he owes?"

"That's the idea."

"Then it'll cost you four thousand."

"Why?"

"Because if you can pull together three so easily, I bet you can scrape up four with a bit more work."

Morrison showed an ugly grin when he heard his partner say that. The teeth he showed were chipped, crooked and tainted a light brown from years of neglect. He wasn't as stupid as he looked, however, because he sensed enough anger coming from Clint to inch his hand toward the holster at his side.

"You really want to do that?" Clint asked as his eyes darted to the other man's gun belt.

Both Dane and Morrison pushed away from the table, standing up so fast that their chairs clattered to the floor behind them. "We'll do what we damn well please," Dane said.

"You keep along this path," Clint warned, "and you won't be able to spend one cent of any money you've collected."

"I suppose you'll see to that, huh?" Dane taunted.

Without a flinch, Clint replied, "In a heartbeat."

There was a crackle of tension hanging in the air between the three of them. Even though there were plenty of other people in that room with them, none of them mattered to the men at that table. Clint's eyes remained cold and unwavering, having already chosen his targets if the lead started to fly. Perhaps sensing that, Dane eased his hand away from his holster.

"You sayin' you can get that money for us?" Dane asked.

Morrison's eyes twitched back and forth between Clint and Dane. Muscles in his face and gun hand twitched beneath his skin, ready for the approaching storm.

"I can see what I can do," Clint offered. "But if you men are just going to wave your guns around and make threats, there's no sense in paying you, is there?"

"You'll fuckin' pay," Morrison snapped.

Without taking his eyes off of Clint, Dane swung one arm out to slap the back of his hand against Dane's chest. "Shut up," he grunted. To Clint, he said, "I ain't just making idle threats."

"I never thought you were," Clint replied calmly.

"That asshole friend of yours borrowed money from us," Dane said as he jabbed a finger at Scott who still sat at his table watching the confrontation. "We aim to get it back."

Still calm, Clint said, "That's fair."

"With interest," Morrison added.

Clint's eyes barely moved as they shifted away from Dane to look at the other man in front of him. The difference in the expression on his face, however, was like day and night.

Instead of cool and calm, Clint seemed cold and deadly when he stared at Morrison and said, "Watch out when you push your luck. You might not like it when you get pushed back."

Morrison wanted to respond to that, but was stopped by a warning grunt from Dane. Instead of spouting more venom in Clint's direction, Morrison said, "You're the one that should watch himself, especially if you're gonna associate yourself with men like that piece of shit over there."

Scott started to walk over, but now it was Clint's turn to keep things from going any farther. He waved at Scott to sit his ass back down.

"Where can I find you gentlemen?" he asked. "After I have a talk with my friend, we'll let you know about the rest."

"He knows where to find us," Dane replied. After that, he walked straight past Clint toward the front door with Morrison trailing not too far behind.

Once those two were gone, everyone else in the place got back to their own business. Clint joined Scott back at their table and asked, "What the hell have you gotten yourself into?"

Chapter Fourteen

Clint and Scott walked along the side of the street, heading for the west end of town. Scott kept his hands jammed into his pockets and his head angled downward, like a young boy who knew he'd been caught doing wrong.

"Sorry, Clint," he said. "I didn't want you to get wrapped up in this part of it."

"Well I am now," Clint replied. Then he punched Scott's shoulder hard enough to make him stagger sideways for his next step.

"What was that for?" Scott groaned.

"It's for not telling me everything. And it's for getting involved with the likes of them two in the first place. Of all people, you should know better than that."

"I do know better. Unfortunately, men like me don't have many other options. I got no rich uncles, no business associates and no banks who look at me very favorably. On account of all that, I need to get my investment money from other places."

"Investment money, huh?"

"That's right. This is a real business for me, Clint. It's an investment."

There have been plenty of times when Scott Meyer had talked about getting into a line of work that didn't involve guns or wearing a mask over his face. Most of those times, he'd spoken of it as a dream or some kind of con. This time was different, Clint could see. This time Scott truly meant what he said, and it seemed as though he wasn't about to jump ship when things got rough.

"Why didn't you come to me?"

"I did," Scott replied. "You were the first person I tried to find once I got things set up in the building I rented and things started coming together."

"No. I mean for the money," Clint said. "Why didn't you come to me for the money you needed?"

"Because I didn't want to owe you any more than I already do."

"What do you owe me?"

Scott stopped and shook his head. Turning slowly to look at him, he said, "My life, Clint. How many times have you saved my life?"

"I don't really keep track of things like that."

"Seven."

"What?" Clint asked with half a laugh.

Scott nodded. "You might not have added them all up, but I did. If it wasn't for you, I would've been dead on seven different occasions."

"Actually, that's not true."

"How do you figure?"

"Because you can only die once," Clint replied with a quick wink.

"You know what I mean."

"Sure I do. Now let's get a better look at this place of yours."

The two of them walked to the building that Scott had purchased with the funds he'd acquired. It was a clean building with windows set into frames that still smelled of freshly cut cedar. There was no door in the frame, so Scott led the way directly inside.

"This is it," he said while opening his arms to encompass the entire store. Walking around a counter that looked to be the oldest thing on the lot, he placed his hands flat upon its warped wooden surface and said, "This is the centerpiece, Clint. It belonged to my father."

"That counter?" Clint asked as he stepped inside.

Scott nodded.

"He used to run a general store in Kansas. Built up a pretty good business without much of any help. My best memories are of him standing behind this counter, cleaning it off and telling me what a terrible mess I'd made of myself."

"That last part doesn't sound too good," Clint said with a wince.

"It was true and he used to say a lot worse stuff about me. That stuff was true too. There were times, though, when he truly wanted to help me be a better man. I was too young and full of piss to listen so I wound up stealing from stores like his instead of working in the one he owned."

Scott's eyes took on a faraway sheen as he stared at the opposite wall. "He always wanted me to take over his store. Told me I had the makings of a hell of a businessman." Snapping himself out of his memories, Scott looked at Clint and added, "He was wrong about that, of course."

"Then why try it now?" Clint asked.

"Abigail . . . you recall me mentioning her?"

"Yeah."

"She thinks I can make something of myself too," Scott said with a hint of pride in his voice. "Thank the Lord she doesn't know how I was when I was younger. Back in my robbing and fighting days, she wouldn't have had a thing to do with me."

"Those days weren't so very long ago, were they?" Clint reminded him.

"A man's gotta start somewhere if he wants to turn himself around."

"That's very true," Clint replied. "And I'm the last one to try and talk you out of something like that. It just seems to me that you don't want her finding out about those days."

"You're damn right I don't."

"That could be a mistake."

Scott's eyes narrowed, showing equal parts suspicion and curiosity.

"Why?"

"Because if she finds out you've been hiding something from her all this time, she'll always wonder what else there is, she doesn't know about you."

"So she'll probably still be suspicious even after I tell her," Scott said.

"For a while, maybe," Clint told him. "Once she finds out you laid it all out for her to see, she'll either love you for it, or walk away. If she decides she can't trust you, you'll lose her for good."

"I don't know which of those is better," Scott said. "Isn't there a way for me to get her for certain?"

"Nope."

"What about a way for me to keep her looking at me the way she does?"

"How's that?" Clint asked.

Scott smiled. "Like I'm a good man."

"Nope. Because you weren't always a good man. Sorry, Scott," Clint went on, with a shrug, "but that's the way it goes. That's the price a man pays for doing the things he does. When a man decides to take up a gun and shoot it at another man or use it to steal or anything else that good men don't do, he's crossed a line. You may decide to step back over and you may even decide never to cross it again, but that doesn't take away the fact that you crossed it in the first place."

Shaking his head, Scott said, "I used to call people childish for whining about somethin' not bein' fair, but this sure as hell isn't fair."

"It's plenty fair," Clint replied. "You were a heller and a robber. Wiping it away like it never happened? Like them dead men weren't killed or those honest men weren't robbed? That wouldn't be fair."

As much as he clearly wanted to be angry with Clint for what he'd said to him, Scott couldn't spark that fire. He could only get himself to a certain point before all of the steam that had been building inside of him drifted away. It left him wilted somewhat and needing to place his hands on the counter for support.

"You want my honest opinion?" Clint asked.

"You mean you haven't been honest yet?" Scott shook his head. "Jesus Christ."

Approaching the counter as if he was Scott's first customer, Clint said, "As long as she knows you're being honest, I'd bet that she wouldn't walk away."

"And if she did?"

"Then you wouldn't want to be with her, anyway."

Scott smiled a bit wider at that.

"Can you tell me something else?" Clint asked.

Scott shrugged his shoulders, as if he didn't have a choice.

"Sure."

"How'd you get this counter all the way out here from Kansas?" Clint asked him.

Chapter Fifteen

The next few days were eventful ones. At least, they were eventful for anyone interested in large quantities of hay, grains and oats. Throughout those days, Scott was kept busy receiving inventory for his store and getting it all squared away inside the two-story building he owned. Whatever didn't fit on the sales floor or in the storage room upstairs was put inside a large shack behind the store.

Clint decided to stay for two reasons. The first one being that Scott truly needed someone he could trust to oversee the process of putting away so much inventory. In a town like Alban that was founded on shipping goods up and down the Mississippi River, that much animal feed was ripe for the plucking of anyone looking to steal something to be tossed onto a boat and sold at pure profit in another town upstream. More than once, Clint found some unsavory types sniffing around the store. He shooed them away easily enough, letting them know that Scott Meyer had at least one friend who carried a gun that was looking out for his interests.

The second reason was the one that surprised him the most. Scott truly wanted to take a run at opening that feed store. This hadn't been the first time he'd been told the story of Scott's father and the store in Kansas. It sure as hell hadn't been the first time Scott had mentioned giving up the outlaw life. It was, however, the first time he'd truly committed to the notion. And if paying to have a sales counter loaded onto a boat, floated to the base of the Mississippi River and then hauled into another town, then Clint didn't know what commitment was.

While Clint may not have been planning on helping to carry stock into a newly opened feed store, a hard day's work was always welcome. When he spotted Hallie walking toward the store, Clint put down the sack of chicken feed he'd been carrying and returned her wave.

"I thought you might be hungry," she said as she approached him.

"I've been around feed all day long," Clint replied. "I can hardly eat another bite."

She made a face and looked at him funny. "You've been sampling the merchandise?"

Passing on the opportunity to make a lewd remark, Clint said, "Just a few oats here and there."

Hallie smiled and nudged him. "And here I thought you'd mention something about getting me alone somewhere to sample what I can give you."

"Me? I would never do such a thing!" Shifting his eyes to the basket Hallie was carrying, Clint asked, "What did you bring me, by the way?"

"A few sandwiches and some pie. Can you take a moment to eat?"

"Sure."

The town was always fairly busy when there were boats at the dock. That morning, two cargo boats arrived and were being unloaded by groups of sailors who shouted back and forth to each other loud enough for Clint to hear at the store. Merchants, travelers and potential customers all roamed the streets as well to see what new goods had come in from along the Mississippi River.

Clint kept his eyes on that crowd as best he could. To some degree, it was a nearly impossible task. The flow of people going to and from the docks on their way to shops or warehouses was moving so swiftly that individual faces were tough to pick out. As he settled onto a stool that was near the store's front door, he studied one of the faces that seemed to be looking in his direction for just a bit too long.

"What's the matter?" Hallie asked.

Squinting at the humanity streaming down the nearby street, Clint said, "Nothing. I thought I recognized someone, that's all."

Hallie leaned toward him so she could kiss Clint on the lips. It was a quick, sweet gesture that made the crowd disappear from Clint's mind.

"I'm here now," she said. "Play your cards right and I'll come back for dessert."

"You mean the pie?" Clint asked.

"No."

That brought a smile to his face.

Chapter Sixteen

The Tres Bouchet wasn't the only place to get a drink in Alban. In fact, when the boats came in, it wasn't even the most crowded. That award would have to go to a saloon called Cajun Charlie's. While it was definitely larger than the Tres Bouchet, its popularity among the men who worked the riverboats could be chalked up to the women who worked at Charlie's. On the surface, they all looked like servers that could be found in any saloon or restaurant. The difference could be seen when someone asked to see the whole menu.

At Cajun Charlie's, the women were on the menu as well and they each carried it with them to show to the customer who asked. Every lady made up her own list of special services and prices which were written on the menu each of them kept. Not every one of those menus were the same. In fact, the variety of things those girls might do was a big part of what kept sailors and locals alike coming back for more.

Charlie's was brimming with customers, most of which were dirty-faced men who smelled of the river. They were seated at tables with women on their laps or standing near the bar where they could look over one menu after another while the ladies whispered into their ears whatever wasn't written on the page. One of those men didn't seem nearly as happy as the others, however. He made his way from one woman to another, talking for a short while before moving on to the next.

Morrison had been to Charlie's plenty of times and it was always hit or miss when it came to how well the women would take to him there. He approached a stout brunette with thick legs and smooth skin and started up another conversation. She listened, showed him her list of services and then listened when he made another request. As politely as she could, she shook her head and walked away once he was finished talking.

Letting out an aggravated sigh, Morrison looked around the place for another prospect. What he found instead was a man watching him intently from one of the few tables in the place that didn't have a woman seated at it. When the man wouldn't look away, Morrison stomped over to his table.

"What the fuck you lookin' at?" he snarled.

"One lonely fellow, if I'm not mistaken," the man replied.

Morrison lunged forward another step, grabbed the man by the front of his shirt and hoisted him to his feet. The man was fairly tall, but lanky and didn't have a lot of weight to him. He came up from his chair easily enough, grinning as Morrison roughly handled him.

"What's so goddamn funny?" Morrison asked.

"Nothing."

"Then stop grinnin' at me before I slap it off your face."

The man took hold of Morrison's wrist and applied a small amount of pressure to the exact spot that sent a jagged surge of pain all the way through Morrison's arm from his elbow to his fingertips. When Morrison retracted his hand and yanked it away, the lanky man said, "You don't seem to be having any luck with these soiled doves."

"Maybe they's just too ugly."

"Or maybe they're not soiled enough?"

Morrison squinted at the lanky man before slowly releasing his grip. "What do you know about that?" he asked.

Dressed in a simple, dark suit, the lanky man dusted it off and smoothed out the places that had been rumpled by Morrison's overzealous hands. Looking Morrison in the eye, he said, "Most of these sailors would be happy enough to have a wet hole they could stick their peckers into. They're too young or eager to know about the finer things where women are concerned."

"Go on."

"There are things they can do, but won't," the lanky man continued. "Things they could do for us, but refuse because they think they're too fucking good to stoop to our level."

Morrison scowled while nodding.

"These bitches are supposed to be up to anything," the lanky man said. "But they still say no when they're asked to do more than just lay down and spread their legs. Every so often, they suck some cock or stick their tongues somewhere they don't normally put them and they think they're God's gift to mankind."

"Yeah," Morrison said. "They're supposed to do whatever they's paid to do."

"Except when it doesn't strike their fancy," the lanky man said. "This is their job. Since when is work supposed to be sunshine and roses every second of every day?"

"That's right!"

Lowering his voice a bit, the lanky man draped an arm around Morrison's shoulder and pulled him in close.

"See that little lady over there in the corner?" he whispered.

Morrison eventually found a short young woman with long brunette hair. She sat alone at her table, drinking wine from a tall glass.

"Yeah," he said.

"She's the one you're after," the lanky man said. "She's up for anything."

"Then why is she alone?"

"Because she frightens away the cowboys and sailors who just want to dip their wicks."

"Usually when a whore's all by herself, it ain't a good thing," Morrison said. "Means they're ugly or mean or somethin' like that."

"She's mean all right," the lanky man said as he nudged Morrison with his elbow. "In all the right ways."

Even though the brunette wasn't the prettiest woman in there, she had a way about her that held Morrison's attention. It was a worldliness that made him think the lanky fellow wasn't just blowing smoke.

Turning to look directly at that man, Morrison asked, "Who the hell are you, anyway? I ain't seen you around here before."

"My name is John Napier. I've been here, but only recently."

"You that whore's pimp?"

"Not at all," Napier replied. "But I do know what I'm talking about. Trust me, she's alone right now because she's an acquired taste. Something tells me, it's a taste you'd enjoy more than the rest of these idiots."

"You get a cut of what she gets paid?"

Before Napier could reply, Morrison caught the brunette's eye. She gave him a look that snagged him deeper than a hook in a fish's mouth.

"Eh, forget it. If she's half as good as you say, I don't give a damn how the money's split." With that, Morrison made his way across the room to where the woman was waiting.

Napier watched from his seat. There was a short conversation between Morrison and the whore, which ended with her patting Morrison's cheek and taking his hand. Even as she led him toward the bedrooms in the back, Morrison looked as though he couldn't believe she'd accepted the offer he'd made.

Raising his drink in a toast, Napier walked over to the bar where a younger girl was standing. She rubbed against him and made her offer. When Napier whispered into her ear, explaining the things he wanted to do to her, the young woman paled and slapped him in the face.

Chapter Seventeen

As promised, the lady Napier had singled out was more than willing to agree to Morrison's request. She barely even flinched when he snarled into her ear about all of the things he wanted to do to her. She smiled weakly, bumped her price up a significant amount and accepted a sum that was still well above the norm of what the other girls in the place would charge.

Her name was Tess, although Morrison would never know because he didn't bother to ask. She led him by the hand to one of the small doors leading from the main room to a narrow hallway. There were three doors on either side of the hall, all of which led to small rooms that were just large enough to contain a cot and a table with a wash basin.

Once inside the room at the end of the hall, Tess tugged the string that laced up the front of her blouse, allowing her ample breasts to emerge from behind the thin fabric.

"Wash up first," she said while dipping a cloth into the basin.

"I paid my money," Morrison said as he threw a few dollars onto the table. "And I didn't pay to take no fucking bath."

She knew better that to argue, fully recognizing the feral hunger etched into Morrison's face.

"All right," she said. "What do you want me to do?"

"Get on yer knees and suck my cock."

She knelt in front of him and pulled open Morrison's pants. His penis was already hard and she took it in one hand while wrapping her lips around its tip. She slowly moved her mouth down to the base of his shaft, sucking and licking every inch of the way. By the time she had him all the way in her mouth, Morrison was letting out a deep sigh.

Much of the angry fire in his belly was gone in that short amount of time. Tess had dealt with plenty of men who liked to talk tough to women. Defusing them was usually a simple matter of weathering the storm at the beginning and getting them to drop their guard. It must have been a long time since this one had been touched by a woman because Morrison was easier to defuse than most.

Morrison placed his hand on top of her head and leaned back, enjoying the way she worked her mouth on him. Just as he was about to catch his breath, she cupped him in one hand while vigorously quickening her pace. Eventually, he tightened his grip on her hair and straightened his stance.

Recognizing that he was about to try and dominate her once more, Tess stood up and pulled open her blouse. His hands went straight to her exposed breasts as if they were the first ones he'd ever seen. Hiking up her skirts, she showed him that she wasn't wearing anything beneath them.

"Is this what you want?" she asked.

"Hell yes it is."

She turned around, lifting her skirts even more. "This is what you want, right?" she purred. "That's what you told me before."

Morrison's eyes were wide as his hand instinctively drifted down to stroke his cock. "Yes."

Crawling onto the bed, Tess reached behind her to find his rigid penis. Although he'd asked for something slightly different when he'd been talking tough in the main room, she guided him to the lips of her pussy.

"There," she said. "You want that."

"I wanna give it to you hard," Morrison snarled. Pressing one hand down on her shoulders, he pushed her face against the mattress and grunted, "And yer gonna take it!"

He was regaining the anger that had been there before. She'd seen it in others who had their reasons for hating women while also wanting to be around them as much as possible. Rather than try to figure out those kinds of men, Tess had done a fairly good job of taming them for just enough time to get their money and send them on their way. What Morrison told her he'd wanted to do wasn't anything Tess hadn't done before. It was just something that was very uncomfortable in a couple different ways. Since she was in a position for him to make a slight adjustment to get what he'd asked for, she decided to take the reins back before things got uncomfortable for her.

"That's all you've got?" she grunted at him. "Come on. Give it to me!"

Rather than pull out and fit himself into a tighter place in her body, Morrison pumped into her pussy harder. "That what you want?" he growled.

Tess arched her back and pulled in a sharp breath. "Oh God, that's too much."

Morrison grabbed onto her hips and pumped into her again, hard. "Not talking so tough now, are ya, bitch? How do ya you like that, huh?"

She gripped the edge of the cot with both hands and looked straight down at the mattress. That way, he couldn't see the complete lack of sincerity on her face when she groaned, "You're so big. Oh, don't be so rough with me."

Morrison slapped her ass and pumped away, not even realizing that her pussy was getting wetter with excitement, in spite of herself.

"Before I finish fuckin' you," he growled, "you're gonna beg for mercy."

"Please," she said blandly. "Go easy."

Grunting like a rutting pig with every breath, Morrison fucked her as hard as he could which was nowhere near Tess's limit. Even so, the noises she made and the squirming she did was so convincing that every one of his angry, hungry urges were sated.

"What's the matter?" he asked breathlessly. "I thought you were a dirty girl."

Turning around to look at him, she replied, "You're too much for me, baby."

As expected, Morrison smiled and thrust into her some more. Sweat dripped down his face and onto his chest. He lifted his chin and pumped between her ample thighs as though he'd truly accomplished something.

Growing tired of him already, Tess pushed her chest down and lifted her rump a bit higher. That way, she could gently wiggle her backside back and forth in time to his rhythm to push him over the edge. It took less than a minute before he started groaning in anticipation.

"God damn," she said, to try to hurry him up. "You're so damn big."

"I know it, bitch. You're gonna keep taking it until I'm through."

"I've never had anyone like you," she moaned.

"Look me in the fucking eyes when you say that, whore."

She turned around again, but her gaze was immediately drawn to something behind her sweaty customer. Her mouth gaped open and a scream formed at the base of her throat.

Standing only a few inches behind Morrison, Napier held a slender blade in one hand. His other hand came up to press a finger to his lips to tell her to hush.

Chapter Eighteen

Morrison didn't even notice the terror on Tess's face. He just continued to pump into her until he felt the bony hand clamp down over his mouth from behind. By the time he realized someone else was in the room there with them, it was too late for Morrison to do a damn thing about it.

Napier's blade was a straight edge razor used in any barber shop in the world. It barely seemed to touch Morrison's skin before it opened him up. The blade swept from one side of his throat to the other, cutting deep and sending a crimson spray over Tess's back and the nearby wall.

When Napier removed his hand from Morrison's mouth, no sound came out. Morrison gulped and gasped for breath. He grabbed for his throat and then stumbled to the side so he could get a look at who stood there behind him. Napier grinned while swatting away the other man's weak attempt to punch him. He laughed when he saw that Morrison's cock was still hard even as its owner dropped to his knees and bled out. Morrison's last act was to grab at his killer one more time, but the attempt was batted aside even easier than the one before it.

"Tell me something," Napier said softly. "Why didn't you scream?"

"I . . . I . . ."

"Sure, I told you stay quiet, but why did you?"

Pulling in a breath, Tess put her back to the wall and pushed herself against it with both feet. Lowering her arms to expose her breasts, she slowly opened her legs to show him her wet pussy.

"I didn't think you'd hurt me," she said. "You've never hurt me before."

"Well, not very much," Napier said. "Not any more than you like."

"That's right. Come here, John. You're the only one who knows what I like."

Napier's smile remained as he unbuttoned his pants and slid them down so he could free his hard cock with one hand. Using the hand that still held the razor, he pushed Tess down onto the cot so he could position himself between her legs.

"It's always better after a kill, isn't it?" he grunted while entering her.

"Yes, baby," she said, opening her legs wide and digging her fingers into his shoulders. "So good."

Napier ran his hand up and down her leg. He then used his other hand do drag the razor's bloody side against her belly, using the flat part of the razor to smear blood all over her exposed flesh. Tess closed her eyes and turned her head so she didn't have to look at it.

He took hold of her legs, propping them against his shoulders so she could lay with her back flat against the cot. Leaning down, he loomed over her while grinding between her thighs. He pumped in and out of her, holding on to one of her breasts as he placed the razor flat against her cheek.

"Look at me," he said.

She pried open her eyes and did her best to look at him without moving too much against the razor.

"I said look at me!" Napier snarled.

"Enough!" Tess said.

When he tried to push into her again, she used both legs to shove him back. As soon as Napier was away from the cot, she jumped to her feet and started gathering her clothes.

"You're going too far," she said. "Killing that asshole is one thing, but don't you try to treat me like I'm another one of them."

Napier hitched up his pants. "I'm sorry, sweetie," he said. "Let me make it up to you."

Smoothing her skirts down, she stood in front of him with her blouse mostly open. She worked the buttons on her blouse as she told him, "You'll clean this up and be quick about it."

"You forgive me?"

"Maybe."

Napier's hand flicked down low and across her belly, slicing the razor through her blouse and several layers of smooth flesh under it.

"How about now?" he asked in an almost tender whisper.

Sliding the blade along the fresh cut he'd made, Napier turned the razor so it scraped against her innards.

"You forgive me now?"

Tess gulped for breath, the movement causing her entire body to flinch. The pain that came from that caused her to twitch even more until her eyes glazed over and she began to fade out of consciousness.

Wrapping one arm around her, Napier lowered her onto the cot. "You wanted to scream when you saw me," he said. "You've been wanting to scream for a while now. Makes you untrustworthy, you see. One of these days, you'll decide to call me out for the things I've done. The things we've done."

Tess's eyes stared blankly at the ceiling, unseeing and unmoving. Her lips quivered and tiny breaths passed back and forth from her mouth.

"Or maybe you wouldn't have said anything," Napier mused as he used the edge of her skirts to wipe off the razor. "Guess we'll never know, will we?"

She shuddered, sucked in one more gasp and was gone.

Napier's eyes roamed over her as his smile became a lecherous sneer. Using the razor to slice away her blouse, he placed a hand on her chest and made two incisions to form an X across her torso.

"Now we can have some real fun."

Chapter Nineteen

The following day, Clint woke up early and got straight to work at Scott's shop. The place was coming together nicely and it was Scott's intention to open up for business by the end of the week. It wouldn't be the prettiest store around, but there would be goods to sell, a counter to greet customers and a register to hold the money. At least, there would be a register just as long as Scott's shipment came when it was supposed to.

Both men had a simple breakfast of oatmeal and coffee before walking to the docks and renting a one-horse cart for the day. Several bags of grain were loaded from a small storehouse onto the cart for the first of many trips back into town. By the afternoon, there were half a dozen piles of grain, corn, chicken feed and oats placed neatly within the store.

Standing at the counter, Scott said, "This place is really lookin' good!"

"You sound surprised," Clint said.

"I guess I wasn't too sure you'd stick around."

"You thought I'd abandon a friend who needs help?"

"No," Scott replied. "I wasn't sure you still thought of me as a friend who deserves to be helped."

"Just try to keep your nose clean for a while this time," Clint told him.

"Something about Mister Meyer that I should know?" asked someone who stood just outside the door on the board-walk.

Clint turned to find Sheriff Tyson outside looking into the store.

"Hello, Sheriff," Clint said. "I've been meaning to have a word with you for a while."

"Have you, now? And here I thought you'd forgotten all about me."

The angry tone in the lawman's voice was impossible to miss. Just to be certain his point was made, he crossed his arms sternly and glared at Clint as though he was about to arrest him.

"This about them old folks that were butchered the other night?" Scott asked.

Tyson nodded. Pointing to Clint, he said, "I'll have a word with you alone."

"Why don't you two use this place for your privacy," Scott offered. "I've got another load to pick up down at the docks. I also wanted to check and see about when my cash register is expected to arrive."

Waiting until Scott had left through the front door, the sheriff stepped inside and looked around.

"Pretty good start for a man like him," the lawman said. "Wonder where he got his money to start it up?"

"Is that what brings you here, Sheriff?" Clint asked. 'Finding out where new merchants get their investors?"

"You know damn well what brings me here. I thought you were going to see about tracking that killer."

"I went back that very night," Clint said. "Got a look at him myself."

"You did?"

"Yeah."

"Then why the hell didn't you tell me about it before now?" Tyson asked.

"Because it wasn't much of a look I got," Clint replied. "I went back that night to see if I'd missed anything."

"That night?"

"Yes."

"Why?" Tyson asked. "Why not wait until morning?"

"Because there might have been more to see. And in the morning, there would be more people out walking around, trampling whatever had been left behind. You ever try to pick out one set of tracks in the middle of one of these streets?"

"All right, so you got a quick look at him," the sheriff said, calming himself. "Tell me about it."

"He's about my height," Clint said. "Skinny. Pale skin. Gaunt features."

"That's it?"

"Yep."

"That's not a lot," Tyson scoffed.

"Which is why I didn't go running back to you to tell you I saw him in the first place," Clint said. He also hadn't wanted to admit to the lawman that the man with knife had outfought him. "Also, we had a scuffle."

Tyson's eyes narrowed. "What kind of scuffle?"

"I chased him. He took a swing at me with a knife. Hell, as far as I'm concerned, the two of us did a hell of a job trampling any tracks I could have seen anyhow. Only thing left in that alley is blood."

"And what have you been doing since then?" Tyson asked.

"I got stitched up and then I've been helping Scott," he said, still not admitting he had come in second best. "It wasn't that long ago, you know. Haven't you been doing anything to find the killer, yourself?"

"Of course I have!" Tyson drew a deep breath and let it out to calm himself. "Truth is," he said while taking a quick glance over his shoulder, "there ain't a lot more to report. I was hoping you had something I could use."

"And I was hoping you'd come to find me sooner to point me in another direction so I could be of some use. Seems like we both hit a dead end."

"Yeah, well maybe you could still find something of use if you keep looking."

"I'll keep my eyes open, but tracking a man in town is different than tracking him out on the range. Out there, you can rely on footprints, broken branches and what's left behind at campsites. In town, you've just got to ask around, be patient and wait for your man to stick his head out."

"This ain't the first man I've tracked either, Adams," Tyson said. "I just don't like waiting around for an animal like this to make himself known. I'd rather hunt him down quick and be done with it."

"I think everyone would prefer that," Clint said. "Hopefully someone saw something and will come to you with it. Until then, I'll see what I can do."

Tyson nodded and walked away.

Before long, Scott made his way back to the store.

"I thought you were going to pick up your shipment," Clint said.

"I will. What did the sheriff want?"

"Weren't you listening from wherever you were lurking?" Clint asked.

His eyes darting to the corner of the building where he'd most likely been keeping out of sight, Scott replied, "Maybe. I thought you would've checked in with him right after you had that scrape with the killer."

"Like I told him, there wasn't much useful to tell."

But even Clint himself thought he should have checked in with the man before now. There wasn't much he could do about it at this point, though. What was done was done.

"And you're worried that he might have something to do with it?" Meyer asked.

"The sheriff?" Clint asked.

"Why not?" Scott replied. "We've both seen enough lawmen to know that most of 'em are crooked in one way or another. This one could be a killer."

Reluctantly, Clint said, "You're right, we both have. But I don't think there's much of a reason for Sheriff Tyson to be involved with this, though. That killer wasn't out to steal money or take anything of value from those old folks—except their lives. If a lawman is gonna get his hands dirty for something, it's most likely one of those two reasons."

"So then you're convinced the sheriff isn't involved?" Meyer said.

"I am, yeah.."

After a few quiet seconds, Scott asked, "Then why does it seem like you're trying not to say something until he gets a little farther away?"

"There's just something strange about that killer," Clint said, shaking his head. "He was so damn calm the whole time we were scrapping in that alley, and he's a hell of a knife fighter. Every time I went for my gun, he had an answer. And then he got the drop on me, and didn't kill me when he had the chance." He shook his head, again. "Strange."

"You mean, even stranger than butchering innocent folks in an alley?"

"Yes. Near as I can tell, there wasn't much of a reason for what he did."

"Sometimes killers are just killers, right?" Scott offered. "Mad dogs that need to be put down."

"He didn't seem like one of those and I should know," Clint said. "I've put down plenty of mad dogs."

"Then what is it?"

"I think he showed up in that alley again, so soon, just to soak it in," Clint said. "I've been thinking it over this whole time, just letting it settle in and I still can't come up with much. That is, unless I'm missing something else about those old folks that were killed."

"I don't think so."

Clint shook his head again, and couldn't seem to stop shaking it.

"And why is nobody talking about the prostitute he also killed? I'm afraid this killer could be something worse than a mad dog," he muttered. "A lot worse."

Chapter Twenty

Since Scott didn't need help in checking his shipments, Clint decided to do some scouting within the town. Whenever there was something as sensational as the Marshall murders happen, most everybody thought they knew something about it. Newspaper stories and rumors replaced actual knowledge and experience until things had a chance to settle down. Once the smoke cleared, the folks who didn't really know anything weren't so quick to throw in their two cents and the ones who did still had their lingering memories.

Clint walked around to several saloons and stores to ask about the Marshalls. While nobody had anything bad to say about the poor old folks who'd been sliced to pieces in that alley, that didn't give Clint much of anything to work with. They had some relatives in nearby towns, but weren't on bad terms with them. They kept to themselves and didn't have a lot of money. Many of the locals barely knew the old timers at all and none of them gave Clint a reason for why they might have been targeted for something so terrible.

That left Clint with one unsettling conclusion: they hadn't been targeted at all.

Even a walk back to that alley didn't spark anything in Clint's head. If he'd come up with anything useful, he would have gone to the sheriff with it immediately. As it stood, he had nothing whatsoever which was frustrating as hell. The more Clint walked around town, the tighter the knot in his stomach became. When he heard the horrified scream coming from down the next street, Clint was actually relieved.

He ran all the way to the source of the scream which was a filthy saloon named Cajun Charlie's. As he got closer to the place, he picked out several shrieking voices wailing at once which explained how he'd heard them from so far away.

Although he hadn't been to the place more than once, Clint knew about Charlie's by reputation alone. It was a stink hole of a cathouse that relied on the variety of whores working there to make up for the rest of its downfalls. The card games were crooked, the beer tasted like skunk piss and the dice were loaded. Yet, despite all of that, Charlie's remained opened and mostly prosperous. Even at that time of the afternoon, Clint found a good number of customers milling around the place when he arrived.

"What is it?" he asked the first person he could find. "What happened here?"

"I don't know," replied a fat man with bloodshot eyes who staggered out through the front door. "Some whore started screamin' and then the rest joined in. Too loud for me."

Pushing past him, Clint stepped inside Cajun Charlie's to find a complete mess. There were women clustered in small groups, some of which were sobbing and others were talking excitedly to one another. A few men gathered at the bar while others stood by their tables to guard the chips stacked at their poker games. Most of the commotion was focused at the entrance to the hallway leading to the back rooms, so that's where Clint headed.

"What happened?" Clint asked.

One of the men, a burly fellow wearing a shoulder holster, extended a hand to push Clint back. "Step away, mister. Ain't your concern."

The instant that man's hand touched his chest, Clint grabbed it and twisted it the wrong way to force the big fellow to step aside. Two other men wearing guns were quick to close in around Clint to hold him back. Two of them grabbed Clint's arms while the third attempted to wrap a beefy arm around his neck.

"Let me go!" Clint shouted.

The man behind the bar jabbed a finger toward Clint and barked, "Get him the hell outta here!"

Despite his best efforts to resist, Clint was dragged toward the front door by the three men. From where he was, Clint could see a few other men standing at the end of the hall. One of the other doors came open, allowing a half-naked woman to run out and race past Clint in a flurry of tears and long blonde hair.

"What happened?" Clint demanded. "Tell me, damn you!"

"Let him go," said Sheriff Tyson as he entered Charlie's and approached the bar. "Then tell both of us what's going on in here."

Chapter Twenty-One

The three men who had hold of Clint weren't quick to let him go. They waited until the bartender gave them a nod before giving in to the lawman's demand. If anything, that gave Clint a glimpse of the power structure inside Alban. For the moment, however, that wasn't what concerned him the most.

Once Clint had been released, Tyson said, "Start talking, Winston."

The barkeep came out from around the bar. He wore trousers and a white shirt that might have been fashionable a few years ago. Now, they were rumpled and stained. The watch chain crossing his midsection was copper and the holster strapped around his waist was well worn. Long, thick sideburns came down to a large chin that made his face resemble that of a tired horse.

"Someone killed one of my girls," Winston said.

"A customer?" Tyson asked.

"Not sure," the barkeep replied. "But one of them was killed too."

"Two people killed?" Clint asked.

Shifting his gaze to Clint, Winston said, "That's right. Who the hell are you?"

"Just answer his question," the sheriff said.

"Two people dead in that room back there. It's a real mess. Looks like a goddamn slaughterhouse. After I got a look, I had to come straight back out here to get a drink."

Tyson pulled in a breath to steel himself. "Do you know what happened?"

Wilson shook his head. "Been busy here as always. The girl that was killed took a customer back to her room and never came out."

"When was that?" Clint asked.

"Last night. I figured he paid extra to spend the whole night with her. That doesn't happen a lot, but it does sometimes."

"Who was the man?"

"Morrison was his name," Winston replied. "Bill, maybe? Sometimes he comes around here with that asshole Dane Miller."

"Where's Dane now?" Clint asked.

"Hell if I know."

As they stood there, the rest of the people who'd been in the hallway walked past them on their way outside. Like most other cathouses, Charlie's smelled of several different things. Perfume, lilac water and sweat were in the mix along with the scents of cigarette smoke and stale liquor coming from the bar. Now that Clint had been there a while, though, a few other scents were coming to his nose. Most powerful among them was the scent of blood.

"Guess we'd better just have a look for ourselves," Clint said.

"Yeah," Tyson said reluctantly. "I guess so."

Both men walked down the hall toward the room at the end. Its door was ajar and, even from a distance, he could see a crimson puddle seeping out like creeping death.

"Jesus Christ," Tyson said once he was able to get a look inside the room.

Clint didn't say anything. He simply didn't have the words needed to describe the carnage contained within those four walls. One body lay on the cot and another was face down on the floor. Both were so badly butchered that it was hard to tell at first glance which was the whore and which was the customer. Reaching for the bandanna around his neck, Clint wrapped it around the lower portion of his face to keep at least some of the smell from reaching down into his throat.

The body on the cot was cut open at the belly. Flaps of skin had been pulled open so wide that the inside of the carcass was on display for all to see. Innards glistened in pools of blood, some of which had been pulled out and dropped onto the cot on either side.

The body on the ground had been sliced open in several different places. Most of the cuts were about eight to twelve inches long and were deep enough to show hints of bone. That one's throat had been cut so deep that the head barely remained attached to the neck. There was so much blood on the cot and floor that it had soaked into the floorboards to form a soft, spongy texture.

Despite the cloth covering his mouth and nose, Clint could barely take a breath without gagging. He and Tyson stepped into the room, being careful not to walk through the largest pools of blood. Since neither of them wanted to inhale unless absolutely necessary, they refrained from speaking while they took a look around.

Both of them began by looking at the bodies, but Clint moved away from them before too long. While Tyson hunkered down to try and look at the face of the corpse on the floor, Clint stooped over to pick up something that had been placed near the door.

"What've you got there?" Tyson asked.

Clint stepped outside of the room and the sheriff was more than willing to follow. Although it didn't smell too much better in the hallway, Clint was able to draw a breath deep enough to fill his lungs. He held up what he'd taken from the room, which was a pair of men's boots.

"This," Clint said, "looks like the reason there isn't a trail of bloody footprints leading away from this room. Apart from ours, that is."

Chapter Twenty-Two

Getting out of that room wasn't enough. Clint had to get out of the entire building before the stench of death even started to come out of his nose. Even then, the odor lingered like a ghost within his skull to remind him of what he'd forced himself to see.

"Her name was Tess," Tyson said. He started to say something else, but had to turn his head away and retch into the closest gutter.

Clint wasn't aware that the lawman had followed him outside until he heard the other man's last meal spill onto the ground. Not even that stink could trump the one that had filled the last room in that dark hallway.

"Whoever did this wasn't an animal," Clint said. "He wasn't no mad dog, no matter how much I'd like him to be."

"You'd like him to be a mad dog?"

Clint nodded slowly. "Mad Dogs are wild. They're quick to anger and make mistakes. All of that makes it easier to put them down. The man who did that," he said while pointing back to Charlie's, "thought things through enough to leave his boots behind rather than leave a trail that could be followed."

"That don't exactly make him smart," the sheriff pointed out. "Common sense is all that is."

"Right. You saw how bad it was in there. Can you imagine how bad it was while those people were being torn apart?"

"He's fast and strong. You said so yourself. That proves it. Any man who could either overpower two folks that way or cut them before they could defend themselves is one hell of a fighter."

"It's more than that, Sheriff. Those two went into that room some time ago and weren't found until just now. That means they've been in there awhile. It also means that when they were killed, it was the middle of the night. That's prime business time for a cathouse."

Tyson's face slowly shifted into an expression of understanding. It had also paled.

"He killed those two without making a sound. And what he did with them—"

"It took time," Clint said. 'He didn't just stab them, kill them and hack them up. He opened them up and did whatever the hell he pleased for a good, long while. And he never got rattled. When he left, he took his boots off, set them down side by side and stepped through the door like just another satisfied customer."

"What could he have done with them in all that time?" Tyson asked. "I mean, I can imagine what he could have done to the woman, but was that all it was?"

"This had nothing to do with rape or even murder. It's a goddamn nightmare is what it is and I don't think there's much rhyme or reason to it."

"How can that be? I mean, we just got finished saying how skilled and tactical he was. Now he's just some bolt of lightning that struck from the blue?"

"He is skilled and he does follow some kind of tactic. But tracking him like we would track anyone else would be a mistake. Perhaps there is rhyme or reason to what he does. It's just nothing we can understand."

"So he's crazy," Tyson said. "At least that makes sense."

Clint shook his head and let his eyes wander around the perimeter of the cathouse. Whatever he was looking for wasn't there, but at least he came up with something. "I have an idea," he said.

"Good, because I'm plumb out of them."

"An animal did this."

"What?"

"You heard me," Clint said. "As far as anyone knows or if anyone asks, it was an animal that did this."

"You mean . . . like a bear?"

"A wild dog or maybe an Indian. Just something along those lines that gives a quick answer to any questions you're asked. Just don't admit to saying anything we've been talking about out here."

Pushing his hat back a bit so he could scratch his head, Sheriff Tyson asked, "Why should I do that? You wanna be the one to tell folks about the real killer?"

"No," Clint said as he closed some of the distance between him and the lawman. "When I went back to that alley, the killer was there too. At the time, I thought he might have been following me because I was working with you but I don't think that's the case. I think he was there to get another look at what he'd done."

"You think he's here now as well?"

"Maybe, but he's going to keep himself hidden better."

"How do you know?"

"Instinct," Clint replied. "If he was just some bloodthirsty lunatic, he wouldn't have been so careful to cover his tracks. As it was, he kept things quiet, he kept them confined to one room and he made certain he couldn't be tracked from that room. A true madman doesn't think that clearly."

"He might," Tyson offered.

"I've seen a few real madmen, sheriff. They're genuine animals and animals aren't so careful."

The sheriff laughed uncomfortably under his breath. "You're getting all of this from some instinct and a pair of left-behind boots?"

"That and from what I saw when I met up with him in that alley. His eyes may have been vicious and a little crazy, but he was no wild man. He wants to make a statement or prove some sort of point. His choice of victims isn't telling us anything."

"How so?" Tyson asked.

"Two whores, an old couple, and a loan shark. What do they have in common?"

"Nothing."

"Exactly. Do you know anything about the whore he killed in the alley?"

"Just that she worked the alleys and streets," Tyson said. "She was just a street whore."

"Then why kill her? It seems like she was first."

"What the hell point could he be trying to prove?" Tyson wondered.

"I don't know that. At least, not yet. I do know he wants to cause fear. Why else would he leave such a gruesome mess behind when he could have killed these same folks any number of ways that were cleaner and quieter?"

"All right, so why not tell folks it was a man? That way, they might be able to keep an eye out for him or let us know if he's been seen around here."

"Because he'll be listening for that," Clint said. "He wants that."

"Why would anyone want that?"

"I don't know, sheriff. What I do know is that we can't try to think like he does or figure out exactly why. The best we can hope for is to steer him to the spot we want him to be so we can catch him as quick as we can."

The lawman snapped his fingers. "Kinda like hunting! Setting bait, figuring where the game is and when to be there."

"Exactly," Clint said. "Just because we don't know exactly what's running through a deer's mind doesn't mean we can't get it to do what we want."

"So . . .he is animal," the lawman chuckled.

"That's right. And we're going to mount the son of a bitch on our wall."

Chapter Twenty-Three

Napier sat at one of the back tables inside the Tres Bouchet, enjoying a bite to eat with one of the Cajun Charlie ladies while all the commotion at Charlie's died down. There was still a heaviness in the air that settled around him like a wool scarf, comforting and itchy at the same time.

The food in front of them was baked chicken and potatoes, poorly cooked and even more poorly seasoned. Picking at the chicken with his fork, Napier asked, "What happened?"

"Didn't you hear about it?" the whore replied. "One of our girls was killed by some Indian."

Napier smirked. "Same Indian that got those two old people the other night?"

"No."

Stopping with his fork raised halfway to his mouth, Napier asked, "What do you mean?"

"Those poor old folks were killed by a wild animal that came in from the riverbed," she told him. "An alligator or maybe some kind of wolf."

"A wolf? That's preposterous. There aren't any wolves around here!"

"Could have been on a boat on its way to a zoo or just snuck on somewhere," she said, "but like I said it could have been an alligator."

"Where did you hear that nonsense?" Napier asked.

"The sheriff's been telling folks as much, on account of the tracker he's got working for him."

"What tracker?"

"Clint Adams. He's the famous Gunsmith. He's worked with lawmen in the roughest towns and he knows what he's talking about. Everyone says so."

Tearing the food from his fork, Napier gnawed on it before stabbing another off his plate. "Everybody, huh?"

"Yes! I hear he and the sheriff have already found who did it," she said.

"I thought you said it was an animal," Napier commented, "not a who."

She shrugged. "Could be both. Either way, Clint Adams can take care of it."

"You talk about him like you know him," Napier said. "Does he get you wet between the legs?"

Blinking at the sudden turn in Napier's tone, she reached out to touch his hand. "It's just exciting, is all. After what happened, someone needs to put an end to it."

"Maybe this Clint Adams doesn't know anything at all."

"Oh, he does," she replied with a sigh. "Just look at him."

Napier snapped his eyes up and asked, "He's here?"

"Yes. Right over there by the bar." She inclined her head. "He just walked in."

Somehow, Napier had been too distracted to see that someone had entered the Tres Bouchet. That wasn't completely surprising since people were coming and going a lot after all the commotion down the street. He smirked to himself when he saw a familiar face at the bar.

Adams stood there, beaming with pride before receiving a grateful hug from one of the whores. They talked for a short while as Adams looked around at the rest of the place. Napier kept calm as Adams looked in his direction. He wasn't completely unprepared for the situation, after all. Napier had smeared just enough dirt onto his face to darken his complexion from the last time he'd met up with Clint Adams. A bulky jacket gave Napier some girth around his body while a loosely tied bandanna hid his neck and the lower portion of his chin.

When Adams glanced at him, Napier let his eyes drift slowly in another direction. He didn't avert his gaze, but instead made it appear disinterested. By the time he glanced back over there, Adams had already gotten back to the whore who seemed to adore him so damn much.

He talked loud and spouted a bunch of nonsense about how the man who'd killed that whore was just some thieving Indian and how the Marshalls were attacked by an animal. And he did it all with a smile on his face. That's what got to Napier the most.

"I have to go," he said to the whore at his table. Apart from the fact that she wasn't gutted like a fish, that one seemed nearly identical to Tess. Not that it mattered, of course.

"Oh," she said. "Will you be back tonight?"

"Maybe."

She said something after that, but Napier had stopped paying attention. He headed for the door and stepped outside at a casual pace. Once he was on the boardwalk, he darted to one side and headed for one of the outhouses situated beside the place.

Sure enough, Clint Adams came straight outside. He looked back and forth, up and down the street, for something that had caught his attention. Perhaps he'd recognized Napier after all. After their first meeting when the blood of those two old timers was still fresh on the ground, Adams sure as hell knew it wasn't some alligator that had ripped open the Marshalls.

That simple thought cleared the fog that had begun creeping into Napier's mind. He smiled broadly and pressed his back against the wall to put him out of sight from anyone on the street. Wedged in there between the Tres Bouchet and the outhouse, he could hear men relieving themselves and smell the shit filling the ditch beneath the smaller structure. Still, he smiled.

"You don't know a goddamn thing," Napier whispered. "This time tomorrow, you'll realize that."

Chapter Twenty-Four

Most of Scott's store was stocked by the next afternoon. He and Clint had been working on it hard enough to do the job of a small team of men and now they were both admiring what had been accomplished.

"Thanks, Clint," Scott said. "Couldn't have done it without you."

"Just remember you owe me," Clint said.

"Name it."

"Free feed whenever I'm in Louisiana."

"Aw hell," Scott groaned. "The way Eclipse puts it away, I might go broke."

"Should've thought about that before you asked for my help," Clint chided.

Scott walked over to the counter where a large cash register now sat. He placed a hand on the metal curves, patting it like it was a beloved cat.

"I'm within spitting distance of opening this place and it's all because of you."

"I'd hardly take credit for all of it" Clint said, "but you're very welcome."

"I'm just surprised you're here and not out there trying to bring in that maniac killer that's running loose."

"If I knew exactly where he was, I'd be there," Clint replied. "Unfortunately, it's like trying to run around in a windstorm to catch a single leaf. It's just better to stand still, be patient and snag the leaf when it eventually flies by."

"Yeah, but it's killin' you to stand still ain't it?"

Without taking any time to consider it, Clint replied. "It is. It really is."

"Then go on and get out there," Scott said. "There ain't much more to do and I can handle it on my own."

"I would, but I don't know where to start. I've already tried walking the streets and looking the normal way."

"What about going back to where them folks were killed?"

"Already did that too. There's just not much to see there apart from blood."

"You ran into him when you went back to that alley," Scott pointed out. "You think you'll run into him again if you just stay in the vicinity of that place or Cajun Charlie's?"

"I've been there whenever I wasn't here," Clint told him. "I've asked around about suspicious men and have gotten a few people describing some skinny fellow with a long face."

"Any names?"

"Yeah. Five of them. Seems the people I talk to are all suspicious of different men or the same man never uses the same name twice. Either way, it doesn't help me much."

"So all that talk of Indians and alligators didn't help?"

Clint took off his hat and rubbed his head.

"That was a shot in the dark. I thought if he was so proud of the terror he'd created, this asshole might show himself if I saw to it that he wasn't going to get any credit for it."

"It was worth a try," Scott offered.

"Sure," Clint replied with a shrug. "If it had worked."

"If it had worked, he would've just come after you."

"That was the idea. I wanted him to come after me so he wouldn't go after anyone else. I may not know what he's thinking, but perhaps I could set up his next target."

"Still tryin' to catch that single leaf in a wind storm, huh?" Scott asked.

"Something like that."

"Well you had a point about standing still for a spell, but there's more to it than that. You gotta be standin' in the right spot."

"True."

"This ain't the right spot, Clint. Get back out there and do what you do."

Clint looked around at the nearly completed store. There was still plenty to be done inside and out, but it had come a long way and was almost ready to accept its first customers.

"What if there isn't much to do until that killer decides to make his next move?" Clint said.

"Then you'll have to be ready for him."

"He could be long gone by now."

"Could be," Scott mused. "I heard tell of an old mountain man that moved around from one town to another slitting the throats of women with curly blonde hair. He never got caught until he just happened to try and kill this one blonde who had five brothers. Only two of them were home when the mountain man came looking, but it was enough."

"What's your point? I should start looking for mountain men?"

"No, it's that if someone wants to kill for no good reason, he'll do it. You can't try to pick out what he's gonna do, exactly, because he might not even know. That mountain man just killed when the mood struck."

"That doesn't make me feel any better," Clint said.

"Wasn't meant to. Maybe you just need to pick a better spot to try and catch your leaf."

"What was that?"

"You know, like you were saying about hunting or catching leaves and whatnot. You've got to find your spot. Ain't like you can hunt from just anywhere. But," Scott added, "you already know that."

Clint jumped to his feet and headed for the door. "I should've known that already," he said on his way out, "but I appreciate the reminder."

Chapter Twenty-Five

Clint moved in a hurry when he left that store. He rushed down the street, looking every way he could as he went. He studied every face, watched every doorway, glanced into every window. By the time he got to where he was going, he felt like a dizzy drunk taking swings at nothing.

His fist pounded against the door of the small square office at the intersection of two of Alban's busiest streets. Before he could knock hard enough to smash the door off its hinges, Sheriff Tyson opened it.

"What's wrong, Clint?" the sheriff asked.

Stepping inside, Clint said, "I just thought of what we need to do to catch this man."

The sheriff's office was the size of a one-room cabin. A desk was in one of the front corners and a rifle cabinet was in the other. At the back of the room was a small stove and a section that had been fenced in by iron bars to form a single jail cell. There was nobody else in the office apart from Clint and Tyson. Even the cell was empty.

"You have an idea?" Tyson said. "I'm listening because I sure as hell can't think of doing anything other than what we've already been doing. To be honest, though, we haven't been doing much."

"We need to draw him out," Clint said.

"I thought that's why you wanted me to spread the word about animals and Indians. Get him riled up. I've been doing that and just about any rumor regarding them killings spreads like a plague."

"We need something more specific. We have to put ourselves in the right spot at the right time."

"We could walk this whole town day and night," Tyson said. "That still leaves plenty of places for this lunatic to be."

Clint took hold of the lawman's shoulders and stared straight into his eyes.

"Listen for a second. We need to arrange something where we know he'll show up, if only for a few seconds."

"And what if he does? You think you can spot him before he slips away?"

"Yes."

Backing away from Clint, Tyson walked over to his desk and sat on its edge.

"What do you have in mind that could draw out an animal like the killer we're after? It would have to be something pretty damn special."

"It will be."

"And how will we know when he shows up?"

"I've seen him once and I can spot him again," Clint replied.

"We've both been scouring every inch of this town as much as we can," Tyson pointed out. "Hell, I've even hired on a few more deputies to lend a hand."

"Really? Where are they?"

"Out and about," the sheriff said. "Doing their best. But they're mostly green young men or weathered men older than me who are better suited to tending a field than hunting a dangerous outlaw. From what I can pay, though, I can't exactly be choosy. To be honest, I'm worried sick that I'll walk around a corner and find one of those men spread open like a dead rabbit in the sun."

"Which is probably what this killer wants."

"You know what he wants? Cause I sure as hell don't."

Clint approached the closest window that looked out onto the street. Staring through the glass, he found himself searching every face as if it could be the one he was after.

"I don't know his reasons and maybe we never will. All I care about is putting an end to him."

"I've been thinking, maybe we've been going about this the wrong way."

Turning to face the lawman, Clint asked, "How so?"

"So far, we've been doing as good as we can," Tyson explained. "We've been doing just what we're supposed to do. But us walking around like we have may be making regular folks feel good, but this killer is one man and all he'd have to do is watch for you, me or my deputies and then turn in the other direction."

"I've thought of that too," Clint sighed. "But anything we do can possibly be the wrong choice. We can't just pull back and let him have the run of this place."

"He could just move on."

Slowly, Clint shook his head. "No. This is where he wants to be. It's his hunting ground."

"That makes it sound like he really is a red-skinned savage."

"He's a predator," Clint said. "Plain and simple. He's killing because he likes it. That's the only thing that makes any sense for what we've seen."

"I've had another thought. It's something I've barely wanted to consider or even say out loud." After a brief hesitation, Tyson said, "He's killed whores, older people, and a criminal. What if he doesn't care who he kills? We could never figure out his next victim."

"If that's the case, then we'll find out for ourselves soon enough when we flush the bastard out."

"I hope so."

"Me too, Sheriff."

Chapter Twenty-Six

Watching the town law walk the streets brought a tranquil smile to Napier's face. It was something like sitting in a quiet room listening to a clock tick. Every little knock from the gears springs came at a precise moment, one after the other, without fail.

The men Tyson had hired as deputies were new to the job. That much could be seen in the way they strutted with their new badges pinned to their shirts, heads held high and hands never straying far from their pistols. Napier spotted them while he was having his supper and as he was on his way inside one of the smaller cathouses in town. He even saw one of them again as he walked down the street to keep an appointment he'd made with Dane Miller.

For a man with such a thick build, Dane carried himself like a frightened little pup. He flinched at every sound while pressing his back against the wall of a general store as though he wanted to push his way inside where he could hide in a corner. As Napier approached, it was all he could do to not look as though he was about to laugh at him.

"What the hell do you want?" Dane snapped.

Holding his hands up to show they were empty, Napier stepped closer and said, "I just wanted to make my delivery."

"Good. Give it here."

Napier reached into an inner jacket pocket to pull out a small bundle of cash. He placed it in Dane's outstretched hand where it was immediately snatched away from him.

"You seem nervous, Dane. What is it?"

"Didn't you hear?" Miller growled. "There's some kinda maniac loose in town."

"And you're worried about being the next victim?"

"Fuck no," Dane spat. "What worries me is the goddamn law strutting around this town and looking into every goddamn corner for this asshole. Makes it near impossible for me to do business anymore."

"My business has been fine," Napier said.

Scowling distastefully, Dane grunted, "Well, that's just fuckin' great for you. Get your grinning face away from me before I stomp my boot into it."

Napier started to walk away, but stopped and turned back around. "I've been doing a lot of business at Cajun Charlie's," he said.

"So? Isn't that where you always do business?"

"Yes and during my time there, I got to see your associate, Mister Morrison. Or, I should say," Napier added with half a smirk, "former associate."

Dane lunged forward to grab Napier by the front of his shirt. "Don't talk about him like that, asshole."

"I'm not trying to speak ill of the dead. I just thought you might like to know that he mentioned you before he and that whore of mine went off to their last night together."

His eyes narrowing, Dane asked, "What did he say?"

"Nothing to me, but he was awfully talkative with Tess."

"Who?"

"Tess," Napier said. "The whore. He was bartering for her services and she raised her price. Mister Morrison told her that money wasn't going to be a problem since he was taking all he needed from you."

Dane released the skinny man with a shove. "Whatever you heard, it wasn't that."

"Oh, I make it my business to keep watch over Tess while she negotiates. That way, I'll know if we're being cheated by a customer afterwards."

"And he told some whore that he was stealing from me?"

Napier shrugged. "Not in those exact words. He did mention something about coming into some money and that it came from you."

"Why the fuck would he talk like that to one of your bitches?" Dane asked.

"My girls can be quite persuasive," Napier said. "It's their job to put men at ease and get them talking. You never know when something useful will slip out. Anyway, I may be mistaken. Perhaps I didn't hear what I thought I heard. It doesn't matter now anyway, right?"

"No. It doesn't. Now get out of my sight."

"Oh, before I go, there's one more thing you might want to know," Napier said.

"Make it quick."

"Do you know someone named Scott Meyer?"

"Yeah," Dane grunted. "He owes me a good chunk of money, plus interest."

"He seems to think that, with Morrison gone, he no longer owes you a cent."

"Is that a fact?" Dane chuckled.

"It is," Napier told him. "And he's been talking about it to several of the girls at Cajun Charlie's and God only knows how many other places around town. In fact, I've heard that he's not the only one of your debtors that seems to think they'll be the ones profiting now that Morrison is dead."

"They know goddamn well that I'm still alive and kicking," Dane snapped.

Napier shrugged. "You've been keeping yourself scarce lately. Maybe you're afraid?"

Dane drew his pistol and jammed its barrel into Napier's stomach. "What the fuck did you just say to me?"

"I'm just the messenger," Napier quickly said. "Isn't that one of the reasons you pay me?"

"What else have you heard, messenger?"

"That's it."

"Find out who else thinks they can get out of paying what they owe to me," Dane growled.

"You can start with Michael Ingels and Abe Hobbs," Napier said. "Those two were shooting their mouths off real good just the other night."

"And why didn't you tell me about it then?"

"Because I wanted to make sure." Also, Napier added sheepishly, "I knew you'd be upset, and that you might . . . shoot the messenger."

"Upset?" Dane sneered. "You're fucking right about that. Where's the last time you saw them two?"

"They frequent Cajun Charlie's and the Tres Bouchet quite a bit. If they're not there—"

"If they ain't there," Dane cut in, "I know where to find 'em. They live on the south end of town."

"I hope you're not thinking about going to see them," Napier said. "Especially with the law walking around making things so difficult for you."

Poking his finger into Napier's chest, Dane said, "Don't you fucking worry about me. I can do what I please and ain't no law dogs can tell me otherwise! You just get back to collecting money from your whores and leave the rest to me."

Napier stepped aside and let Dane storm past him. As he watched Dane charge toward the street, Napier smiled contentedly. The sight of clockwork going through its motions made him feel warm inside.

Chapter Twenty-Seven

Clint spent the better part of the rest of that day collecting things he needed for the plan he'd created to draw out the man they were calling the Butcher of the Bayou. It hadn't been long since the bodies were discovered in Cajun Charlie's, but word had spread quicker than smoke in a wind storm about every grisly detail. As more rumors were passed, some of the details became even more gruesome than they'd been in reality. Considering the carnage that Clint had seen, that was quite a feat.

For a while, the locals seemed to be buying the stories that Clint and Sheriff Tyson had been spreading about the killings being the work of a wild animal and Indians. While the tactic didn't seem to do much of anything to anger the killer enough to slip up, it did even less for the rest of the town. A few people bought what they were told, but that didn't last long before folks settled on one monstrous killer and named him The Butcher of the Bayou.

Clint winced when he'd first heard that name. Now that the killer had a title, he would probably be feeling pretty good about himself. Since he seemed to be able to move around however he pleased after committing such vile acts, a bit of pride wasn't exactly out of line.

That notion burrowed deep under Clint's skin as he quietly went about his business and collected the supplies he needed. As the sun made its way to the horizon, the plan he'd concocted seemed less likely to work. By the time night fell, it felt damn near preposterous.

Having acquired what he was after, Clint made his way to the Tres Bouchet for a late supper. Seeing Hallie's face light up when she spotted him coming in through the front door went a long way in relieving the tension that gripped his neck and shoulders.

"Clint!" she said. Using a quick series of nods toward one of the empty tables, she quickened her steps while trying not to drop the plates in her hands. "Sit right over there. I'll come over as soon as I can."

The table she'd offered was against a back wall with a straight view at the front window. He couldn't see the entire street from there, but someone outside couldn't get a clean shot at him, either. Normally, the latter was his main concern. Now, he felt twitchy whenever he couldn't see everything around him. Listening to the instincts that had kept him alive this far, Clint put his back to a wall and kept his gun within easy reach.

While Clint took his seat, Hallie delivered the plates in her hand to one of the tables closer to the window. She spoke with them for a few seconds and hastily broke away so she could cross to the back of the room.

Smiling while wiping some of the grease from her hands, she pulled out the chair next to Clint and sat down. In an excited chatter, she said, "I heard you've taken a job as one of Sheriff Tyson's deputies."

"Don't believe everything you hear," he told her.

"You mean about the wild animals killing old folks in alleyways?"

Shrugging, he said, "That, too."

"I don't know how long that was supposed to last. After nobody spotted anything bigger than a mangy dog running around here, that story dried up. Have you been helping to find the Butcher?"

"Don't call him that."

"Why not?" Recoiling slightly, Hallie asked, "Are you mad at me?"

"No," Clint replied in a gentler tone. "Just tired. The sheriff and I have been walking our legs off, searching every inch of this town whenever we can and have come up with nothing to show for it."

"So you're not a deputy?"

"Not exactly."

"That means you're not getting paid?"

"Yeah," Clint sighed. "No pay, and no badge."

"So why are you doing this?" When she saw the look Clint gave her, Hallie added, "You're risking your life by trying to hunt down a killer, aren't you? Even if it is just some wild animal or Indian, they're still dangerous. You barely know anyone in this town."

"Does that mean I should just sit back and do nothing if I might have a chance to bring this animal down?"

"No. It means that if you're putting your neck on the chopping block to help, more people around here should be helping you." She looked around at the people sitting at the tables who were either eating, playing cards or talking with one of the working girls who drifted in and out of the Tres Bouchet. "As much as the men around here like to talk about those killings, they don't seem to care enough to do anything about them."

"This is a port town," Clint said. "Places like this tend to be rougher than most."

"I suppose so. Just turns my stomach sometimes knowing that most men won't lift a finger to do anything unless it puts money in their pockets or directly affects their families. Even then, if there's a chance they might get hurt, they'll keep their heads down and wait for the storm to pass. I've seen it too many times."

Clint placed his hand on top of hers. "So have I," he said. "That's why I've decided not to be one of those men."

"Perhaps you could set a good example."

"Perhaps. Mostly I do it so I can look at myself in the mirror."

She smiled at Clint and held on to his hand. "You must have tracked a lot of killers like this one."

"Not like this one. The more I try to think about what could be driving this man, the less sense it makes to me. I've asked folks around here about those old timers from the alley, about Morrison and that woman from Charlie's, and none of it connects. None of it makes any sense."

"Evil doesn't have to make sense to us," she whispered as though she might be nervous about attracting the attention of demons.

"Even someone who kills for sport wouldn't leave something behind like what we found," Clint said. "There was no challenge in killing those old folks, if that was what he was after. There was nothing taken from the bodies. There was still plenty of cash in Morrison's pockets, for Christ's sake, so money wasn't a reason."

"It was two terrible things that happened," she offered. "Maybe there's just not much to see."

"It's more than that. There's also what I saw when I went back to that alley. He was just there. Just . . . watching. I don't think he was following me or even knew I was coming."

"He's a wicked, evil person. That's it."

"No!" Clint said as he slammed his fist down onto the table.

Some of the others in the place looked in his direction, but not for long. There had been too much going on in town for one outburst to hold them for long.

"There's got to be a reason for all of this," Clint said.

"Why is it so hard to believe a devil can exist? A devil kills for no reason at all."

"If there isn't a reason," Clint explained, "or any sort of pattern, then there's no chance of catching this man. I'll just have to wait for someone else to get torn apart. I've seen what was left behind in both of these killings. If another one happens and there was anything at all I could've done to stop it, I'll be partly to blame for it."

"I wish I could help you, Clint."

"I know."

"Is there anything I can do?" Hallie asked hopefully.

"Keep your eyes open. If you see anything strange or hear anything that seems peculiar, let me know. Right now, anything at all might turn the tide."

She smiled, patted his hand and gave Clint a kiss on the cheek. It didn't solve all his problems, but it made him feel a little better. All things considered, that wasn't a bad thing.

Chapter Twenty-Eight

Normally, Sheriff Tyson's office was fairly empty. Apart from him, there was only one deputy who patrolled the streets of Alban. Recently, however, he'd taken on a bunch of fresh faces until the killer known as The Butcher of the Bayou was caught and made to pay for his crimes. While the added manpower was welcome, the sheriff didn't particularly enjoy the added work that came along with it.

"All of you, quiet!" Tyson hollered, his voice filling the confines of his little office. Nearly a dozen men were crammed into the office, most of which hadn't even seen the inside of the place until that day.

Some of the men respected the sheriff's command while others took a few moments to finish their chatter with one another. Eventually, the office was calm enough for one man to be heard above all the others without shouting.

"Have any of you found anything useful?" Tyson asked.

"You mean at Cajun Charlie's?" one of the fresh deputies asked.

"Yeah."

"There's a man there steering business away from other cathouses to some of the whores he shares profits with. I think he sells opium too."

"How is that useful?"

"He worked with Dane Miller and that fella Morrison, who was killed."

"Does he know anything about the killings?" Tyson said.

"No."

"Are you certain?"

"Yes. I questioned him myself."

"Anyone else?"

Nobody had much to say.

"Fine," Tyson sighed. "I think it's time we try something else. How many of you have any tracking experience?"

A few of the men raised their hands.

"You men are staying on to form a posse," Tyson announced. "There will be extra pay. Not a lot, but it'll be something. The rest of you, go on home and come back here if you think of anything to offer."

"You're cutting us loose?" asked the man who'd spoken up about the pimp he'd discovered.

"Pretty much, yeah. You all did a fine job and I'll let you know if you're needed again. I'm sure you will be once we organize a group to string this bastard up like he deserves."

That got a rousing cheer from a good portion of the men who seemed more than happy to be done with their brief time as peace keepers. All of the men filed toward the door, except for one who lingered before turning back around. Once it was just him and the sheriff in the office, the young man cleared his throat to catch Tyson's attention.

The man was in his early twenties with close-cropped blond hair and a face that had been baked in the Louisiana sun. He was also the one who'd voiced his concern about the man he'd discovered at Cajun Charlie's.

"You got something more to say?" Tyson asked.

"Yes sir, Sheriff. I do."

"What's your name again?"

"Daniel, sir. Daniel Bass."

"Were you in the Army?"

"Yes sir," Bass replied.

"Well you're not in it right now. No need to call me sir. What can I do for you?"

"There was something else I wanted to say. Something I didn't want to mention in front of them others."

"What's that, Daniel?"

"I think I know who killed Morrison and that whore."

Chapter Twenty-Nine

Clint walked into the sheriff's office and shut the door behind him. "I'm almost ready," he announced. "All we need to do is—" He stopped before finishing his sentence, noticing that there was an unexpected guest in the office along with the lawman. "What the hell is he doing here?" Clint asked.

Sheriff Tyson was smiling from ear to ear. He walked up to Clint, slapped him on the back and said, "We've got our man. After turning the town upside down, we forced him into slipping up just like we hoped we would."

Clint looked at the sheriff and then at the man who stood inside the small cage built into one of the back corners of the office.

"That's not him."

"You're goddamn right it ain't me," Dane Miller said from behind the iron bars. "I didn't kill nobody!"

"Shut the hell up!" Tyson barked. To Clint, he said, "Step outside with me where we can talk."

Once they were outside, Clint pointed back to the door of the office and the cell within while asking, "What the hell is going on?"

"We did it!" Tyson declared.

"I saw the killer with my own eyes and it wasn't him."

"What you saw was someone who seemed like he might be the killer."

"It was him," Clint said.

"Why? Because he told you so? There could be any number of reasons why someone would spout off like that. The first of which is that he's just some loon looking to become a known bad man."

Clint shook his head. "That wasn't it. What makes you think Dane could slice those people apart like that?"

"He's got a reason. One of the men that was working for me was keeping watch on Cajun Charlie's and he heard Dane grousing about how his old partner Morrison had cheated him out of money and how Tess was one of the whores working for him through some other fella in town."

"And that means he cut them into ribbons?" Clint asked.

"I've seen men killed for a lot less and I'd wager you have, too."

"What about those old folks?" Clint asked. "Why would Dane want to harm them?"

"Same reason. Money."

"What?"

"They owed him and Morrison money that was used to purchase land they needed to build a new house. They hadn't paid anything to him for months."

Clint shook his head while pacing in front of the office door. "And where did this deputy of yours come by this information?"

"That actually came from one of the other men I'd hired," Tyson said. "Daniel was talking with him and put two and two together. Seems that two of the other folks who owed Dane and Morrison money heard Dane talking about how much he wanted to start cleaning house, starting with his partner and going all the way through to them who'd fallen behind on payments."

"That doesn't make a lick of sense," Clint said.

"It's enough for me to hold Dane in my cell for a while until I figure this out. What if there's even a chance that he's the man we're after?"

"But he's not!"

Holding his hands in a placating gesture, Tyson said, "We both kicked around the idea that there could be more than one killer in these parts. Perhaps Dane is one and the man you saw is the other?"

Too frustrated to stand there any longer, Clint said, "Where do I find these other men?"

"Which ones?"

"The ones your deputies spoke to! The ones who owed money who told whatever story they did to convince you to toss the wrong man into a cell and call it a day!" Clint roared.

"Their names are Abe Hobbs and Michael Ingels," Tyson said. "I was meaning to go over there myself, but I thought I'd put Dane somewhere he couldn't escape if all this proved to be true."

"Let's go."

Chapter Thirty

Abe Hobbs and Michael Ingels lived like anyone would expect for men who had to borrow money from scum to survive. What few possessions they had were contained in filthy little shacks on the edge of town. Remnants from their last few meals were stuck to dented tin plates or rotting in little trash heaps outside their doors. Other than that, both men had something else in common.

They were both dead.

Neither of them looked to have left this world with much fanfare. Hobbs sat in a chair, his head hanging down and his arms hanging to the sides with a couple of gaping bullet wounds in his chest. Ingels was sprawled on his floor with one hand burnt to a crisp after falling into his fireplace. Three bullet holes had been drilled through his face.

Upon finding Hobbs first, Clint and Tyson hurried over to Ingels's place to discover his corpse. Squatting down next to Ingels, Clint touched the dead man's neck with the back of his hand.

"Still pretty warm," Clint said. "Just like Hobbs."

"So both of them weren't killed very long ago," the sheriff said. "Probably around the same time. Looks like Dane was busy after all."

"What makes you so sure it was him?"

"Makes sense. Both of these men owed Dane money. Also, Dane was accused of the other killings." Shrugging, the sheriff added, "Where there's smoke, there's fire."

Clint stood up and started looking around the squalid little home. "Why don't you think this could be the man I saw in that alley?"

"Because," Tyson said while motioning toward the body on the floor, "look for yourself. This ain't anything like them others."

"It's a murder," Clint said. "The man we're after is a murderer."

The lawman sighed. "How long have you been in Alban?"

"What does that matter?"

"How long, Clint?"

"Not long. Why?"

"Because these ain't exactly the first killings in this town," Tyson said. "Between the saloons and sailors, there's shootings and drownings more often than I like. Then you take into account the unsavory types that drift in and out of any town that has river money flowing through it and you get even more bodies to toss onto the pile."

"I've been in plenty of tough towns," Clint said sternly. "I've seen plenty of killings. You're telling me that the ones we've seen are just like the rest?"

"Of course not."

"And you honestly think Dane Miller could have gunned these men down like this?"

"Honestly? Yes. I do."

Clint looked down at the body of Michael Ingels. Sadly enough, he'd seen plenty of others like it himself and knew there would be plenty more to come. Ingels and Hobbs suffered common deaths in a violent land. Dane Miller was a common brute in that same world.

"Yeah," Clint admitted. "I suppose it does make sense that Dane killed these two."

Seemingly relieved by Clint's statement, the sheriff slid his hat back on his head so he could swipe at his brow.

"I think Hobbs had some family in New Orleans. As for Ingels, I'm not so sure."

"Then maybe Ingels could be the one to do some good. At least for us, anyway."

"What are you talking about?" Before Clint had a chance to answer, Tyson put the pieces together for himself. "No! You want to use him for what we had in mind?"

"It would work out better than the original plan. Besides, it doesn't seem like there's anyone to mourn him here."

Tyson looked down at Ingels.

"Mike was kind of a jackass, but I don't know. Would he get a proper burial afterwards?"

"Of course."

You really think it'll do some good?"

"There's only one way to find out," Clint replied.

Chapter Thirty-One

"Another one's been slaughtered!" shouted a man with a pale face and thick, greasy hair. "The Butcher's got another one!"

Almost immediately, people came to answer the frantic call. Although they all tried to look as if they were frightened and appalled by what they might see, all of them were still very eager to see it. One of the most eager to see what was going on also happened to be best at hiding the anxiousness he felt.

John Napier stood outside the Tres Bouchet, having a whispered conversation with one of his whores about how she should approach a group of sailors to squeeze the most money out of them. When he heard the cry coming from just a short way down the street, his ears perked up and he turned to look over his shoulder.

"Oh God," gasped the whore in front of him. She was a short girl with chestnut brown hair and a generous bosom. "I thought the Butcher was caught already."

"I hear he's still out and free as a bird," chimed in one of the customers. "They'll never catch that devil."

Although he heard those voices around him, Napier barely regarded them as anything other than noises in the distance. His eyes narrowed into slits as if to block out every other thing in his vicinity other than what he was searching for.

He didn't find anything at all until a young woman raced around the corner down the street, her arms flailing as if she was drowning in a deep pool and trying to swim to the surface.

"It's terrible!" she cried. "It's horrible. Oh God!"

Napier jumped down from the boardwalk and charged at her. She was so disoriented that she didn't' even realize he was coming until Napier was close enough to reach out and grab her with both hands. The girl's feet skidded against the dirt. Her hand lashed out wildly at him and her face contorted even more than it already had been.

Expertly slapping away her reflexive attempts to hit him, Napier avoided getting caught by her fingernails and grabbed her wrist before she could take another swing.

"What is it?" he hissed. "What did you see?"

"Let me go!"

"Answer me, girl!"

But the young woman was too frantic to form a coherent thought, much less put that thought into words. Her breaths came in desperate gulps, causing her chest to swell and contract like a set of bellows. The more Napier tried to reach her, the more the young woman struggled to get away from him.

Napier's next instinct was to slap her across the face. Not only did he want to catch her attention, but the temptation to strike the squirming female was almost too much to resist. Before he could act on that impulse, more people clustered in around them.

"What did you see?" one of them asked.

"What happened?" asked another.

"Are you all right?"

"Was it the Butcher?"

"Where is he?"

"Quiet!" Napier roared. "All of you!"

Everyone fell silent.

Taking hold of the young woman with both hands on her shoulders, Napier looked her in the eyes and told her a bold-faced lie without so much as a twitch.

"You're safe now. Everything will be just fine."

Like all the other sheep before her, the young woman believed what she was told and took comfort from it.

"What did you see?" he asked.

"A body," she whispered in a voice that was quiet enough to bring everyone else closer to her so they might hear. "A dead person."

"Who is it?"

Shaking her head, she replied, "I don't know. I couldn't tell. There was so much blood."

"Where is it?" Napier pressed. "Can you take me there?"

"Yes, but I don't want to."

"Show us where it is, darling," said one of the local men who'd come to see what was going on.

Reluctantly, the young woman nodded and pointed to a patch of dark shadows down an empty street.

Chapter Thirty-Two

Another alley, another body.

Only this one wasn't his work.

The girl showed him to the alley, and then ran off. He let her go because he didn't need her anymore. There was a crowd in front of the alley, talking amongst themselves about how this was another victim of the Butcher of the Bayou. When he'd pushed his way to the front he saw the man lying there, with bullet holes in his chest.

How could anyone imagine that a murder like this . . . this artless killing was his?

And then he got it.

He backed away from the mouth of the alley and looked around. It was a trap and he had walked right into it!

***

From his rooftop Clint watched the crowd in front of the alley where he and the sheriff had left the body of Mike Ingels. He knew he desperately needed to spot the man he had fought with before the Butcher realized this was a trap. And he would, Clint had no doubt of that. The man was too smart not to pick up on it once he saw the body. Clint's only hope was the spot him, and get down to the street fast enough to catch him.

There was a good crowd on the street, but he managed to eye a girl who was leading a man there. She pointed out the alley, and then ran off, apparently to spread the news further. She turned out to be an important aide to Clint and Sheriff Tyson, even though they didn't know her.

As the slender man worked his way to the front of the crowd, Clint hurried down from the roof. He knew as soon as the man saw the body, he would know it was a trap.

The sheriff was on the ground, across from the crowd. He didn't know what to watch for, but he was ready for Clint to tell him.

When Clint got down to the street he knew he was a split second too late. The slender man had worked his way out through the crowd, and was running off down the street.

"There he goes!" Clint shouted to Tyson, and took off after him.

***

Napier didn't see Clint Adams, but he heard him, and he knew he was behind him. He knew the street was too crowded for Adams—whose identity he had learned by now—to shoot at him, for fear of hitting an innocent bystander.

He took a knife from his belt, and as he passed those innocents, he reached out and sliced into them, leaving behind him a collection of injured bystanders.

Clint could see the blood on the ground, being left by the thin man in his wake. He could see the man ahead of him, running easily, slashing innocents as he went. As Clint ran by them he could see they were not seriously injured, so he didn't stop. And he didn't use his gun, not for fear of injuring more of those bystanders, but because he wanted to talk to this killer. He wanted to find out the whys of what he was doing.

Clint felt there had to be a reason for the killings.

***

Napier felt exhilarated. The possibility of getting caught by the Gunsmith and having to kill him was almost too much to bear. If he had only known who he was that first time he could have killed him, then. Now, it would be taking too much of a chance, because he knew the sheriff had to be behind Adams, both chasing him. And maybe even some of those inept deputies.

He cut down an alley, knowing he was taking a chance, since the innocent bystanders were on the streets. But he knew something Clint Adams didn't know, because he had been here before.

Adams would be surprised.

***

Clint saw the man turn into an alley, off the main street. Maybe he should just draw his gun and shoot him down, forget about his questions.

But when he turned down the alley to follow, he saw that it was empty, even though it came to a dead end.

Behind him, Sheriff Tyson caught up, turned into the alley and joined him.

"Where'd he go?" the lawman asked, breathlessly.

"He turned into here," Clint said.

"A dead end?"

Clint nodded.

"There," Tyson said, pointing to the one door in the alley. "He must've gone in there."

"Come on."

Clint and the sheriff approached the door together. When they tried the knob, they found the door unlocked. Clint opened the door and they went in together, the sheriff with his gun in his hand. They found themselves in a room filled with children seated at desks, all of them either staring at Clint and the sheriff, or toward the front of the room. Whichever way they were looking, they were wide-eyed.

"Damn," Clint said.

"A school," Tyson said.

In the front of the room stood their mad dog killer, the Butcher, with his arms around a woman who had to be the children's teacher.

He was holding a straight razor to her throat.

Chapter Thirty-Three

"Hello, gents," the man said. "Meet Miss Willis. She's the school marm here." Miss Willis' head was hiding Napier's face.

"Now, take it easy . . ." Sheriff Tyson said.

"I was gonna give you the same advice, Sheriff," the man said. "Why don't you put that gun away? Just holster it, that's all I ask."

Tyson hesitated, and Clint said, "You better do what he says."

"Can't you take him?" Tyson asked.

"Too many kids," Clint said. "And that's a sharp razor he's got to Miss Willis' neck."

Tyson holstered his gun.

"There you go, now we can all relax some—oh, except for Miss Willis, here." He tapped her neck with the edge of the razor he was holding. "She really can't relax too well."

Miss Willis' eyes were glazed as she gasped, "Help . . . don't let him hurt the . . . the children . . ."

"Oh, I ain't gonna hurt the kids," the man said. "I ain't killed any kids yet, have I, Adams?"

"Not that we know of."

"Naw," the killer said, "not yet . . . but we ain't got time to talk about that now. Gents, I'm gonna need you to stay right where you are while me and Miss Willis, here, take our leave out that door behind me."

"We can't let you just walk out!" Tysom blustered.

"Sure you can," the man said, "unless you want a dead teacher and, maybe, some dead kids."

Clint was somewhat surprised that all the kids—who looked to range from 5 to 15—were sitting quietly. Apparently, they all knew the danger they—and their teacher--were facing.

"Kids," the killer said, "the word on the street is that this here is the famous Gunsmith."

All the kids turned to look at Clint.

"And he's gonna let me walk out of here," the man went on. "Me and Miss Willis."

Miss Willis was a pretty woman in her 30's, and Clint didn't want to be the reason she got sliced, or killed.

"Go ahead," Clint said, "walk out. We won't stop you. Not now. But we found you once, and we'll find you again."

"Ah, but I got careless this time, and you got lucky," the killer said. "Both of those things ain't gonna happen again at the same time."

"We'll see," Clint said.

"Come on, sweetie," the killer said, to Miss Willis, "we're gonna back up to this door and go out, and if you drag your feet, I'm gonna have to cut you. Understand?"

"I . . . understand."

"Let's go." He started moving backwards. "See you, gents."

When they reached the door he had her open it, and then they went through it and closed it firmly.

"Go out through the alley, Sheriff," Clint said. "Maybe you can catch him coming out. I'll follow them."

"Right!" The sheriff drew his gun and ran back out the door they had come in.

"Kids," Clint said, moving toward the door at the front of the room, "just stay in your seats until I come back with Miss Willis."

"Don't let him kill our teacher!" one kid shouted.

I'm going to do my best, he thought, but what he shouted back was, "I won't."

***

After they left the classroom the killer said to Miss Willis, "I don't want to go out the front door. Is there another way out of here?"

"Yes," she said, "there's a back door—"

He pressed the edge of the razor tighter against her smooth throat and said, "Show me!"

"You—you're not going to kill me, are you?" she asked.

"Not if you cooperate," he said. "Now show me the way out."

Chapter Thirty-Four

When Clint went out the front door the sheriff was there waiting for him.

"Nothing?" he asked.

"Not a sign of 'em," Tyson said.

"There's got to be another way out," Clint said. "Come on."

They went back inside, ran into a man in his 50's, wearing a three piece suit who was coming down the hall.

"What's the meaning of this?" the man demanded.

"Who are you?" Tyson asked.

"I'm the principal, here—"

"You better get somebody into Miss Willis' class to watch those kids--and keep them inside. There's a killer loose in the building."

"Oh, my," the man said. "Not the Butcher—"

"Just go!" Tyson snapped.

"Is there another way out of here?" Clint asked the man, before he went.

"A back door," the principal said, "Down that hall and to the left."

"Let's go!" Tyson said.

They followed the principal's directions and found the back door. As they burst through it they literally tripped over the school teacher, who was on the ground in front of them.

"Check on her," Clint said. "I'll see if I can catch him."

But it was no use. The killer was gone, and they still knew nothing more about him than they had known before.

Clint returned to where the sheriff was leaning over the school teacher.

"Is she dead?" he asked.

"No," Tyson said. "It looks like she . . . just fainted."

"Let's take her inside."

Clint picked her up in his arms and carried her back into the building.

***

After they made sure the school teacher was all right, and had nothing to tell them— "He didn't say a word to me, and I . . . I fainted like a school girl."—they left the school and went to the sheriff's office.

Tyson poured them each a glass of whiskey and they sat, he behind his desk, and Clint in front of it.

"Goddamn it!" the lawman swore. "The trap worked, and we've got nothin' to show for it."

"You didn't recognize him?" Clint asked.

"I didn't get a good look at his face."

"We've got one thing," Clint said.

"What can that possibly be?"

"He didn't kill Miss Willis," Clint said. "Why not?"

"Who knows," Tyson said. "You think you do?"

"I think it proves he's not quite as mad as he'd have people believe," Clint said. "He could've killed her, but he had no reason to."

"Say, that's right," Tyson said. "He could've killed her for no good reason at all, yet he didn't."

"So," Clint said, "we know something about him now that we didn't know before."

"And how does that help us find him?" the sheriff asked.

"I don't know," Clint admitted. "I just don't know."

***

Clint turned down another glass of whiskey and left the sheriff's office. The lawman was going to check in with his deputies, but didn't expect to get anything from them.

Clint thought he would go back to Scott Meyer's store and see what was happening there. Then maybe he would go and check in with Hallie.

***

Napier was feeling a thrill he hadn't felt in some time.

He had gotten away from Adams and the sheriff, and he was sure he had confused the hell out of them by not killing the teacher. It was all he could do not to, though. She smelled so sweet and felt so good in his arms, he had just been raring to tear at her flesh.

But he knew that leaving her alive was something the men chasing him would just not understand.

He hadn't gone far after leaving the schoolhouse. He had taken refuge in a doorway and watched as Clint Adams came running out after him, looked up and down the street, and then walked back to the school with his shoulders slumped.

Napier left the safety of the doorway and followed Adams back to the school. When the Gunsmith went in the back door, Napier circled around and waited out front.

He followed Adams and the sheriff back to the lawman's office, sand now he was following the Gunsmith to wherever he was going. He was hoping Adams would lead him to his hotel.

Instead, the Gunsmith stopped at what looked like a feed store—a new feed store.

Napier took up position across the street.

***

Clint entered the store, saw Scott Meyer talking with a man who had money in his hand. The money passed, and the two men shook hands. Then the customer left.

"That was my first customer," Scott said, showing Clint the money.

"That's good."

"You don't look to happy," Scott said, tucking the money into his pocket. "What happened?"

Clint explained.

"I'm sorry to hear all that," Scott said, when Clint finished. "Maybe I can help—"

"No," Clint said. "You need to stay here and run your store. You made a sale over your father's counter, Scott. That's a big deal, right?"

"Thanks," Scott said, "but like I said, I couldn't have done it without you."

"Look," Clint said, "I've got some things to do. I'll be back later. You can close and we'll get some supper."

"Deal."

Clint nodded, turned and left the store.

***

Across the street Napier saw Clint leave, thought for a moment about following him again, but he didn't want to push his luck. He had gone this far without Adams seeing him. Instead, he decided to go across the street and see who was in the store, and what Clint Adams' connection to it was.

He stepped out of the doorway and crossed the street.

***

Scott looked up from his father's counter when another man entered the store. He was tall, slender, had a big smile on his face.

"New store?" he asked.

"Brand new," Scott said. "My name's Scott Meyer."

"Yours?"

"All mine."

"I saw a man leaving," the man said, "thought I recognized him."

"Oh?"

"Somebody famous," the thin man said. "the Gunsmith?"

"That was Clint Adams," Scott said. "He's a real good friend of mine."

"And partner?"

"No," Scott said, "he's been helpful, but no, we ain't partners."

The man looked around.

"Well, now" he said, "I may be in the market for some feed . . . .

As Scott Meyer turned his back to point to the different kinds of feed he was carrying, Napier took his razor out of his pocket and snapped it open.

Chapter Thirty-Five

Clint went to Tres Bouchet to see Hallie.

"Do you want a table?" she asked.

"Not now," he said. "I'll come back later with Scott."

"Then what do you want?" she asked.

He gave her a look and said, "You."

She grinned.

"Right here?"

He looked around at the customers in the place. They were eating, drinking, talking and, at one table in a corner, playing cards. No one was paying any attention to them.

"Well," he said, "not right here. Is there another room . . . a hallway?"

"You're serious?" she asked. "What's happened?"

"I almost had him Hallie," Clint said. "I lured him out, chased him, and almost had him."

"What happened?"

"He went into a school, grabbed a teacher, used her as a hostage."

"What about the kids?"

"All safe."

"Well, that's good." She put aside the towel she had been holding and placed her hands on her hips. "There is."

"What?"

"A hallway."

He smiled.

"Show me."

***

Napier left the feed store, feeling lighter than air. He had enjoyed all the work he had done with his razor, but this . . . this feed store would be different.

This building would go up in flames in a heartbeat.

***

Hallie told the kitchen staff she'd be away for half-an-hour, then took Clint by the hand. She led him to the back of the room, through a doorway, into a hallway.

"This is a hallway, all right."

She reached for his belt.

"Can we lock that door?" he asked.

"No," she said, undoing his belt, "doesn't that make it more exciting?"

"Hallie—"

"You need this, don't you?" she asked.

"Yes, I do."

"Then let's not waste time," she said. "We've got about twenty-eight minutes."

She finished with his belt, waited for him to remove his gunbelt, which he slung over his shoulders, and then lowered his trousers and underwear. She grabbed his cock and stroked it until it was good and hard, then put her back against the wall, reached down and raised her dress.

"The underwear—" he started to say.

"Rip it!" she said.

She didn't have to tell him twice. He grabbed it with one hand and tore it off, tossed it down the hallway. Then he slid his hands beneath her bare ass and lifted her up, lowered her down onto his cock. He slid in nice and easy because she was so wet.

"Oh God," she gasped, "I needed this, too."

Clint wasn't concerned about that. He was after what he needed, a major release of the tension in his body. It was those kids in the school room. He'd had no guarantee that he was going to be able to get them all out alive, let alone the teacher.

Hallie wrapped her arms around his neck and held on tightly while he continued to raise and lower her on his pole. He never came out, just moved in and out of her without ever leaving her.

"Oh Clint," she gasped, squeezing her eyes shut.

He began moving her faster up and down on him, grunting and moving his hips in unison with the movement.

He couldn't afford to miss catching this killer again. When he got him within shooting distance again, he was going to take care of him. Never mind finding out why he had done what he'd done. It was time to put him down.

Clint gritted his teeth, firmed his jaw as his time came. When he exploded inside of her, it was all he could do not to let out a huge bellow of pleasure.

Hallie buried her face in his neck, pressed her mouth up against him to muffle her own cries.

"Jesus," she said, smoothing down the front of her dress. "That's a first for me."

"Sex standing up?" he asked.

"No," she said, "sex with a man still wearing a gun."

He took the gun off his shoulder and strapped it back on, now that his pants were back up.

"Did that help you?" she asked.

"Yes," he said, "a lot."

"Good," she said. "It helped me, too. But now I have to go back to work."

"I'll be back later," he said, "with Scott Meyer."

"For steaks?" she asked.

"For steaks."

"I'll have them ready," she promised.

She kissed him, and they left the hallway.

***

Hours later a waiter was walking up that hallway, found the torn underwear on the floor, raised it to his nose, then happily stuffed it into his pocket.

Chapter Thirty-Six

Clint left the Tres Bouchet, but found that after sex in the hall, he wanted a drink. He walked to Cajun Charlie's. Something drew him there. He entered, walked to the bar and ordered a beer. Once he sipped it, he knew that wasn't the draw.

What was?

He turned to face the room and looked around. Gambling and girls. He knew some people considered this a salon, others identified it as a cathouse. And since two whores had been killed, maybe this was a place to get started—again.

He turned back to the bar, called the bartender over.

"The whore who was killed by the Butcher," he said.

"In the alley?"

Clint shook his head.

"The other one."

"Ah," the man said, "Tess."

"She worked here."

The bartender, a burly man in his 50's, nodded and said, "Yeah, She did. Sometimes."

"Sometimes?"

"Well," the man said, "she had a room upstairs, but she didn't always use it."

"So when she uses it, you get a piece."

"Right."

"And when she doesn't?"

"I don't."

"Who's her pimp?" Clint asked. "You?"

"When she's here, sort of," the man said. "But she's got another."

"Who?"

"A man named Napier."

"And where do I find him?"

The bartender stared at him for a few seconds before answering.

"You're the Gunsmith, right?"

"That's right."

"You're used to dealin' with gunfighters," he said, "and Indians, comancheros, people like that."

"Right."

"Well, this is Alban," the bartender said. "Louisiana. You might as well be in New Orleans. It's different. And Napier, he's different."

"What are you telling me?" Clint asked.

"He's crazy," the bartender said. "But he's smart. You ain't never dealt with anybody like him, before. And he moves like a ghost."

"Actually," Clint said, "maybe I have. Can you tell me where to find him?"

"Well, usually, right here."

"Is he here now?"

"No. In fact, I ain't seen him here since Tess was killed."

"Maybe he's in mourning," Clint said.

"Ha!" the bartender said. "A man would have to have feelin's to be in mournmin'."

"And he doesn't?"

"He's as cold as ice," the bartender said, "even when he has a smile on his face."

"What's he look like?" Clint asked.

"You wouldn't think he's much if you saw him," the bartender said, "until you saw him in action."

"Action?"

"I've never seen him lose a bar fight."

"Is that his specialty?"

"His specialty is takin' care of his girls," the barman said. "That's what makes his reaction to Tess bein' killed odd."

"Why so?"

"He's not that upset about it," the man said, "and she was his best girl. Tess would do just about anythin' for money."

Clint finished his beer and put the empty on the bar.

"I'll be back tonight," he said. "If you see him, don't tell him I was asking about him."

"I won't."

Clint gave the man a hard stare.

"If he knows, I'll know who told him."

"Oh, don't worry about me," the bartender said. "I've got no reason to like John Napier, believe me."

"I will," Clint said, "later."

Chapter Thirty-Seven

Clint left Cajun Charlie's and headed back to the sheriff's office. When he walked in, Tyson didn't look happy. He was sitting behind his desk, drinking from a coffee mug.

"Coffee or whiskey?" Clint asked, approaching the desk.

"Both," Tyson answered. "It started out as more coffee, but now it's more whiskey. Want one?"

"No," Clint said, seating himself. "I just had a beer at Cajun Charlie's."

"You drank that swill and you're still alive? What were you doin' there?"

"Something I should have done a long time ago," Clint said. "Asking the bartender questions."

"Any good answers?"

"Do you know man named Napier?"

"A pimp," the lawman said. "Just like any other pimp."

"Maybe not."

Tyson sat forward in his chair, put his mug down on the desk top. "You think John Napier is the Butcher?"

"It's possible," Clint said. "I'll just have to get a look at him to find out."

"And when do you intend to do that?"

"Tonight," Clint sad, "hopefully at Cajun Charlie's."

"Fine, let's go."

"Oh, not now," Clint said, putting his hand out to stop the lawman from standing. "I just came from there. No, I'm going to supper first, with my friend, Scott Meyer. After that, I'll head over to Charlie's."

"Fine, then," Tyson said, settling back in his seat. "I'll meet you there."

"What about your deputies? Anything?"

"Nope," Tyson said, "that was a waste of time and money."

Clint stood and headed for the door.

"We'll be eating at Tres Bouchet, if you get hungry."

"The way my stomach's been since these murders started, I ain't been hungry in a dog's age."

"Suit yourself." Clint opened the office door. "See you later."

***

He walked from the sheriff's office to Scott's feed store and, curiously, found the front door locked. He knocked on it, but there was no answer. He peered through the window. The interior seemed quiet. If something was wrong, it hadn't had any effect on the store, itself.

He tried forcing the door, but Scott had built it very well. He considered breaking a window, but that would cost Scott money to replace, if it turned out nothing was wrong. And, truthfully, what could be wrong? Scott was not involved in any way in the search for the Butcher of the Bayou.

He remembered Scott had built a back door into the structure, so he went down the side alley to the rear of the building to try it.

The back door was solid wood, no window, and harder to force than the front. Clint pounded on it hard, and just when he was about to give up, it popped open.

He opened the door slowly with his left hand, keeping his right free and near his gun. Stepping inside, he closed the door behind him, and latched it. It had popped open because it hadn't been latched.

He found himself in a back storeroom, with bags of feed and grain all around him. It had started to get dark outside, so he waited for his eyes to adjust. When it did he found a lamp and lit it.

Holding the lamp he went to the doorway and held it out in front of him. It was the interior of the store. Maybe Scott had left and gone to Tres Bouchet to wait for him.

"Scott?" he called. "Scott, are you here . . . somewhere?"

No answer.

Before leaving by the back door he recalled that Scott had built himself an office extension. It was behind the counter, and had a heavy wooden door. For all Clint knew, the room could have been almost soundproof.

He went behind the counter to the door, considered knocking on it, then decided, to hell with it, and just slammed it open, his gun hand ready (to the Gunsmith having his gun hand "ready" was the same as anyone else having their gun in their hands).

For a moment he thought the office was empty, but then he saw the feet sticking out from behind the desk. Momentarily panicked that his friend was dead, he noticed that there was no odor of blood. He hurried around behind the desk, and found Scott Meyer—alive, and trussed up!

Chapter Thirty-Eight

Clint untied Scott and got him into his desk chair.

"What the hell happened?" he asked.

"Beats me," Scott replied, rubbing the back of his head. "Last I remember I was talking to a customer and bam, it went dark. I woke tied up back here."

"Who was the customer?"

"I don't know," Scott said. "He walked in off the street and we started takin'."

"About what?"

"Well, you, at first," Scott said. "He said he saw you leave, thought he knew you."

"What did he look like, Scott?"

"A thin fella, kinda squirly. Had sort of an odd look in his eyes. He said he needed a lot of feed, and then . . . I guess he hit me when I turned." He rubbed his head, again. "Why would he do that?"

"Because," Clint said, "that was him, the killer."

"The Butcher?" Scott's eyes went wide? "Then why didn't he kill me?"

Clint sniffed the air, looked over at the door and saw smoke coming from the crack beneath it.

"I think I know."

Napier knew Clint Adams would show up, eventually. He left the back door unlatched, and as soon as the Gunsmith went inside, he started the fire.

He slipped inside by the back door—which he had figured out how to unlatch from the outside—and crept through the storeroom to the main part of the store. He knew whatever he put a match to in there would burn, so he started with the counter, and the shelves behind it. Then he went around and quickly set fire to bags of feed and grain. Finally, he went into the storeroom again, lit up the stock of feed and grain bags, and slipped out the back door.

He was right. The place went up like a stack of dry twigs.

"Fire?" Scott said. "Jesus! My place."

"Can you stand?" Clint asked.

"Damn it, yeah." Scott stood up. "Let's get this fire put out!"

He rushed to the door, but Clint said, "Wait, wait!"

But Scott was beyond waiting. He reached for the door, and Clint moved. He tackled Scott, driving him out of the way of the opening door, and the flash of flames that came through it.

Suddenly, the interior of the office was in engulfed, including the desk Scott had just been seated at. All of the new wood of the extension was ripe for the flames.

"Christ!" Scott said. "Where's the fire brigade?"

"This fire is beyond putting out, Scott," Clint shouted, above the sound of crackling flame. "What we need to do now is get out alive!"

They looked around the room. There was no other way out. No door, no windows. Scott had built the room to be a small fortress for himself. Now it was might end up being his tomb, along with Clint.

"What's behind that wall?" Clint asked, pointing behind the desk.

"Nothin'," Scott shouted. "The outside."

"Can we break it down?"

"Not with our bare hands."

"What about the roof?"

Scott looked up at the roof, which was already ablaze.

"Same thing," he said. "We'd need somethin', like an axe, to get through these walls or the roof."

Both men began to cough, their eyes burning. Clint was starting to think they were simply going to have to run through the flames and hope for the best, when he felt something beneath his feet.

"What about the floor?" he asked. "What's underneath?"

"A crawlspace!"

Clint could feel that the boards beneath his feet had some give in them.

"We've got to get these boards up!" Clint said.

They fell to their knees, beneath the flames and the smoke that filled the air above them.

Scott turned and looked at his desk, which was completely in flames, and the chair behind it. It was a chair he had ordered special from back east.

"The chair!" he said, pointing.

It was a leather swivel chair, with metal arms and wheels.

They both ran to it, lifted it up and smashed it down on the floor, again, and again, until it was in pieces. Then they grabbed the metal arms and used them to pry up a board from the floor, then another and another, until there was enough room.

"Can we get to the outside under there?" Clint asked.

"We should."

Clint grabbed the front of Scott's shirt.

"If we get trapped for any reason, Scott, we're dead," Clint told him.

"We're dead, anyway."

That was true. The flames were now burning them, and the smoke was choking them. It was now or never.

Clint slid down into the hole first, followed closely by a choking Scott.

Chapter Thirty-Nine

By the time Clint and Scott crawled out from under the burning buildings, the fire brigade was there. But Clint's assessment had been true. The building was beyond saving. The old wood and new wood had gone up like kindling, as well as the bags of feed and grain.

Choking, their eyes tearing, they stood there and watched as the roof collapsed.

"What the hell happened?"

Clint turned, saw Sheriff Tyson.

"The Butcher," Clint said. "He set fire to the place, trapping us inside."

"How'd you get out?"

"Crawled underneath."

"You're lucky you made it out alive."

"Yeah," Clint said, "but he's not."

The three men stood shoulder-to-shoulder, watching with a gathering crowd as the fire brigade gave up. Clint looked around, wondered if the Butcher was in the crowd, watching.

"What was I thinkin'?" Scott said.

"What?" Clint asked.

"What the hell was I thinkin'?" Scott said, again. "Did I really think I could start a business?"

"This isn't your fault, Scott," Clint said, putting his hand on his friend's shoulder. He was going to say, "If it's anybody's fault, it's mine," but Scott spoke first.

"No," Scott said, "but it's my luck, ain't it?" He looked at Clint. "I should probably stick to what I know. Thievin' and gamblin'."

"You need to recover from this," Clint said. "Go home. Get cleaned up, have a good night's sleep. Meet me at my hotel tomorrow morning."

"Yeah," Scott said. "A good night's sleep."

He turned and walked off, his shoulders slumped, his feet dragging.

Tyson moved over to stand next to Clint.

"What are you gonna do now?" Tyson asked.

"I'm going to go to my hotel," Clint told him, "get myself cleaned up, and then go to Cajun Charlie's to take a look at this man, Napier."

"John Napier."

"Right," Clint said.

"The pimp."

"He may be a pimp," Clint said, "but he might also be the Butcher of the Bayou."

"And if he is, you'll tell me, right?"

Clint turned his head and looked at the sheriff.

"Yes," he said, "I'll tell you."

Sheriff Tyson waggled a forefinger in front of Clint's nose.

"It would not be a good idea to take the law into your own hands, Adams," he warned.

"Now why would I do a thing like that?" Clint asked.

John Napier watched the store burn.

He stood back from the crowd, in the shadows, so no one could see him.

While the fire burned uncontrollably, he experienced a feeling of great power, especially knowing that the Gunsmith was trapped inside.

Then, when he saw Adams and his friend crawl out from under the burning structure, he smiled and shook his head. Of course, it wouldn't be that easy to kill the Gunsmith. He was going to have to do it, himself.

He watched as the Gunsmith, his friend and the sheriff stood together, watching the fire. He enjoyed cutting people with his razor, but he was also enjoying watching this raging fire that he had set.

What would it be like to set an entire block on fire?

Or an entire town?

Chapter Forty

Clint knew he should probably take a bath, but he decided to leave that for the next day. He wanted to get over to Cajun Charlie's.

When he got to Charlie's there was even more activity than there had been before. He went to the bar, made room for himself, and got the bartender's attention.

"You're back," the man said. "Another beer?"

"No," Clint said, "I barely survived the last one. Is he here?"

"Who, Napier?"

"Did we talk about anyone else?"

"No, he ain't been here. Not yet, anyway."

"Are any of his girls here?"

The bartender waved his arm.

"Take your pick," he said. "They're all his."

"Not yours?"

"Oh, no," he said, "Napier wouldn't allow that."

Odd, earlier the bartender said they were his, sometimes. Clint decided to take everything this man said with a grain of salt.

"Why do you allow Napier to do business in your place?" Clint asked.

"Hey, friend," the man said, "I'm just the bartender, re-member?"

"Really?" Clint asked. "I had the feeling you were the owner."

"I was the owner," he said. "Not no more."

"Napier?"

"Oh, no," he said, "Napier don't own the place, but he thinks he does."

Before Clint could ask anything else the bartender was called away to the other end of the bar. It would be a while before he could get back to Clint.

"You here alone, handsome?"

Clint turned, saw that the girl who was talking to him had black hair, dark eyes, full lips, and a long, slinky body in a blue dress. She was one of Cajun Charlie's many attractive girls.

"I am alone," he said, "but I'm waiting to meet a friend, a fella named Napier. You know him?"

She made a face, moved further away from him.

"Yeah, I know 'im. He's a friend of yours?"

He saw he would lose her if he answered yes.

"Well," he said, "an acquaintance, really. I can't say as I actually like him."

She got closer now, put her hand on his left arm.

"You smell kinda smoky," she said. "I like it."

"Thanks," he said, "I like the way you smell, too."

"Ya wanna sit at a table with me?" she asked. "Have a drink?"

"Sure."

"Come on." She tugged on his arm, led him to a table he didn't like.

"How about that one?" he asked, pointing,

"That's against the wall."

"I know," he said." I want to be able to see the whole place."

"Whatever you say, darlin'." She led him to the table he'd chosen. "Have a seat, I'll get the drinks. What'll ya have?"

Clint said, "Beer," in spite of himself.

"Comin' up."

She made her way through the crowd, back to the bar. Clint was able to make out most of the floor, and from his vantage point he could see the front doors.

The girl came back with his beer and what looked like a glass of champagne for herself. She sat across from him and pushed his dirty mug of beer over to him.

"What's your name?" he asked her.

"Vanessa."

"Vanessa, did you know Tess? The girl who was killed?"

"Tess." The girl sat back, looking as if she'd been punched in the stomach. "She was my best friend. Why'd you ask about her?"

"I'm trying to find out who killed her."

"The Butcher killed 'er," she said. "That's what they're sayin'."

"Yes, but I want to find out who the Butcher is. Do you have any idea?"

"Me? Why would I know?" She drank some champagne. "Are you the law?"

"No," he said. "I'm just trying to help a friend of mine."

"And he knew Tess?"

"No, but he's been hurt by the Butcher, too."

"Hurt?" she said, looking confused. "I thought he was just killin' people."

"He is," Clint said. "He tried to kill my friend."

"He tried to kill John Napier?"

"No," Clint said, "a real friend. Napier just might have some information for me."

"Mister, if I was you I wouldn't believe anythin' John Napier had to say," she said. Then she suddenly looked worried "Hey, you ain't gonna tell 'im I said that, are you?"

"Not a word," Clint said. "I promise."

She looked relieved.

"Thanks."

"Is he your pimp?"

"No, but he wants to be," she said. "I keep puttin' him off, but before long I'll give in."

"Why?"

"Because ya gotta give in to Napier if you wanna make a living in Alban."

"Well," Clint said, "maybe that won't be true for much longer."

Chapter Forty-One

Since it seemed obvious to Vanessa that her new friend was not friends with John Napier, but was intending to take him on, she decided to play her trade elsewhere, with some-body who didn't have a death wish. Besides, the word had gone around that the Gunsmith was in town asking questions about the Butcher. She had the feeling this was him.

Clint thought it was just as well that she moved on. He didn't need to worry about her getting hurt, if it came to some deadly action between he and the killer.

As the time clicked by Clint was starting to think that, after the fire, maybe Napier had gone into hiding. On the other hand, who would think to blame the Butcher of the Bayou for a fire? His specialty was cutting people up.

Finally, after a couple of hours of nursing the same dirty beer, the batwing doors swung inward and John Napier walked in. At least, he thought it was John Napier. It <u>was</u> the knife fighter he had tangled with in the alley, the man he had chased into the schoolhouse. However, what he could not say for sure was that it was the man who had been christened "the Butcher of the Bayou," or that it was the man who had set the fire. He hadn't actually seen him do any of those things.

Which all meant that he could not just up and shoot the man on sight, more's the pity. If and when he killed him, he needed to be able to prove that he was the Butcher of the Bayou.

He watched the man stop just inside the room and scan it with his eyes. He was careful, that was obvious. There was an almost imperceptible nod that passed between Napier and the bartender, giving Clint the idea again that he might not have been getting the straight story from the barman. That was okay. Now that he saw the man in the light, he knew that this was the Butcher. Now all he had to do was prove it or catch him in the act.

Clint sat back and waited. He had an idea about how this was going to go. Napier had to have been at the fire, to admire his handiwork. That meant he would have seen Clint and Scott escape from the building. This meant he knew Scott could identify him, if not as the man who had set the fire, then as the last man he saw before he was knocked out and the fire was set. Napier was going to have to make a move.

Finally, he spotted Clint and strolled casually across the room to his table.

"Mr. Adams."

"I presume you're Napier," Clint said.

"In the flesh." The man pointed at the empty chair. "Mind if I sit?"

"That's actually my preference," Clint said.

Napier sat. Clint now clearly recognized him as the man he'd tangled with twice already.

"I see you're smart enough not to drink the beer, here," Napier said. "Wiser to stick with whiskey from a previously unopened bottle."

"The glasses are probably still dirty."

"I can handle that," Napier said, and waved a hand.

Clint wasn't sure who he had waved to, but in moments one of the girls—not Vanessa, but a small, almost chubby girl—appeared with an unopened bottle and two shiny, clean glasses.

"Thank you, Gina," he said.

She nodded nervously and backed away.

"One of your girls?" Clint asked.

"They're all my girls."

"Do they all know that?"

Napier smiled.

"They will," the man said, "eventually."

He opened the bottle, poured two glasses of whiskey and pushed one across the table at Clint.

"Why don't we drink to your escape?" Napier asked. "That was a close call you and your friend had."

"I figured you were there, somewhere. In the crowd?"

"Across the street," Napier said. "I don't like crowds." He tossed off his whiskey, poured another.

"Why are we here, drinking whiskey?" Clint asked him.

"Well, it's better than the alternative, don't you think?" Napier asked. "Trying to kill one another?"

"I assume you have your razor with you."

"And you certainly have your gun," Napier said. "You could shoot me dead right now without any problem."

"Except that I'd go to prison for murder, since there's no proof you did anything."

Napier smiled.

"But wouldn't it be worth it, knowing you got me off the street? And the people of Alban were safe?"

"No," Clint said.

"Then, on the other hand, why don't you just leave?" he asked. "Take your friend with you. I give you his life, as a gift. Or is there a woman you like. Take her. Leave Alban to me."

"I can't do that, either."

"Then that leaves us sitting here, drinking whiskey." He refilled Clint's glass. "Out of clean glasses, I assure you."

"I need a third option," Clint said.

"Then you'll have you make one up," Napier said, "because I'm not giving you one."

"Well, now that you're here, in front of me," Clint said, "why don't I just have you watched all the time?"

"By who?" Napier asked. "The sheriff? His so-called deputies? Private detectives?" Napier shook his head. "None of them would survive. This is now between you and me, Mr. Adams."

"Is that what this was about?" Clint asked. "You and me."

"Oh, no," Napier said. "This had nothing to do with you, until you decided to get involved. But now it's between you and me."

Clint's eyes strayed across the floor to the bartender, who was watching them.

"There's got to be a third party," Clint said, shifting his eyes back to Napier. "Someone who knows you, knows what you are and can testify to it."

"There was such a person," Napier said, seeming sad, "but she's gone now."

"Tess?"

"What do you know about Tess?" Napier asked.

"Just that she was one of your girls and she was murdered. I suppose she was your—what? accomplice for a while? But finally she had to go?"

"Tess was . . . dear to me for some time," Napier said. "But I can't afford such feelings."

"I see." Clint looked at the bartender. "So there's no one else you're close to."

"No one."

"No one left who would lie for you."

Napier smiled.

"You're thinking of one of these girls? Gina, perhaps? Or Vanessa?"

"I wouldn't put one of these girls in that danger," Clint said.

"How gallant of you." Napier poured another whiskey. He went to pour one for Clint, who held his hand over the glass.

"I've had enough."

Napier put the bottle down, picked up his own drink.

"Then where does that leave us?"

"I have to kill you," Clint said, "but in such a way that I won't go to jail for it."

"So somewhere on the street you'll shoot me in the back?"

"Doing that would destroy me as a man," Clint said, "and then I might as well be in jail—or dead."

"So then, maybe you can sacrifice yourself?"

Clint shook his head.

"You're limiting your options, Mr. Adams," Napier said, "whereas, I never limit mine." He leaned forward. "There's nothing I wouldn't do, which gives me a huge advantage over you."

Clint thought about drawing his gun and shooting the man there and then. What could he say to the sheriff? That Napier threatened him with his razor blade? He looked around. There would be no witnesses. No one was looking at them, except for the bartender, and he'd just say Clint did it in cold blood.

Napier sat back.

"One of us should stand up and leave," he said, "and since I belong here, and you don't . . ."

Clint didn't respond. He simply stood up and left the saloon.

Chapter Forty-Two

Out in front of Charlie's Clint encountered Sheriff Tyson, who was apparently about to enter.

"Is he in there?" he asked.

"He is," Clint said. "I just had a drink with him."

"And you didn't kill 'im?"

"I can't prove he killed any of those people, or set the fire," Clint said.

"You ain't a judge," Tyson said. "You don't have to prove it. Is he the fella you fought with in the alley?"

"Yes."

"And chased through the schoolhouse?"

"Yes."

Tyson shrugged.

"Then kill 'im," the lawman said. "I ain't gonna arrest you, and you can just leave town."

"But you'll have to justify yourself in court, later," Clint said. "I can't leave you to do that."

Tyson looked annoyed.

"Goddamnit, you make a good point."

"Right," Clint said. "You're a lawman. Whatever we do, you've got to be able to justify it."

"I'm still havin' a hard time believin' it's Napier," he said. "He's been a fixture here for years, as a pimp. What made him go over the edge?"

"I think," Clint said, "the person to put that question to might be the bartender inside."

"Ed Mitchum?" Tyson asked. "Why?"

"I just have this feeling there's a . . . connection," Clint said.

"Mitchum's a bartender, pure and simple," the lawman said. "That's all he's ever been."

"And Napier's only ever been a pimp," Clint pointed out. "Maybe, together, they've become a monster."

"Well," Tyson said, "we can go in and talk to Mitchum right now."

"No," Clint said, putting his hand out to keep the man from entering the salon, "Napier is still in there. Let's leave that for tomorrow, when we can get him alone."

"Okay. But what about tonight?"

"Tonight," Clint said, "I've got to take care of a sick friend."

***

His sick friend was Scott Meyer, and he sat with him in a small saloon called The Whiskey Barrel, near the docks.

"Why here?" Clint had asked.

"Because this is where I belong," Scott said.

"Scott—"

"Naw, naw," Scott said, waving Clint's words off drunkenly, "look at my luck, Clint. I got my place built up, stocked, and had my first customer, and what happens?"

"A madman burns it down," Clint said. "That's got nothing to do with your luck?"

"Oh, no? What's it got to do with, then?"

"A crazy man," Clint said, "a crazy man who I'm going to take care of."

"Why don't you just leave town?" Scott asked. "Go! Leave me and the town to our bad luck. Leave the crazed killer to the law."

"I can't do that to either one of you," Clint said. "Napier and I have now made this personal."

"Well," Scott said, pouring himself another whiskey, "do that, then, and leave me to drink myself to the bottom of this bottle."

"Scott," Clint said, "you can rebuild."

"That takes money," Scott said, "and I've used all my money and all my credit up."

"I'll back you."

"You've got the money?"

"I do," Clint said. "We'll go to the bank and get it, and you can start rebuilding."

Scott sat back in his chair.

"You'd do that for me?"

"I would."

"Why?"

"Because we're friends."

Scott waited a moment, then said, "No, we ain't friends—"

"Scott—"

"—I'll only take the money if we're partners." He put his hand out.

Clint shook Scott Meyer's hand and said, "Partners!"

Chapter Forty-Three

Clint's decision to back Scott in rebuilding his business was not all about friendship, it was also about guilt. It was he who brought Scott Meyer into John Napier's world. It was his faulty Napier decided to kill Scott along with Clint in that fire. Napier was dabbling in not only murder, but mind games, as well. But Clint had played such games with murderers before, some of them clever Indians, others simply men who thought they were smarter than he was. And they may have been, but, in the end, they didn't win.

And neither would Napier.

***

Napier remained at his table as Clint left and worked on his whiskey bottle. The bartender, Mitchum, kept looking over, but he just shook his head. There was no reason for them to talk now. That would come later.

He scanned the room, looking for a likely target, but in fact he wasn't in the mood for killing tonight. He was in the mood for drinking, and thinking. He thought the fire would have taken care of his Clint Adams problem, but Adams proved resilient. It was pretty obvious that he was going to have to take care of killing the Gunsmith himself, hands on.

When he saw Gina he waved her over.

"Yeah, boss?" she said.

"Sit."

Gingerly, she sat across from him. She was in her mid-20's, and Napier made her nervous.

"Did you see the man I was just sitting here with?"

"Yeah, so?"

"Know who he was?"

"The word went around that he's the Gunsmith," she said.

"Was he talking with anyone else before I came in?"

"Yeah," Gina said, "Vanessa sat with him. He bought her some champagne."

"Did they sit together long?"

"No," Gina said. "In fact, she didn't even finish her champagne before she got up and moved on."

"Maybe because she found out who he was?"

"Maybe."

"Ask her," Napier said, "and get back to me."

She thought about asking him why he didn't ask her, but didn't dare question him.

"Okay."

She got up and went to find Vanessa.

***

Despite the fact that he'd offered to back Scott Meyer's business and the man had accepted, Scott continued to drink. But he claimed it was now a celebration. In any case, Clint had to practically carry the man back to his boarding house and put him to bed.

He had to knock on the door, which was opened by a spinsterish woman in her 50's who said she owned the place. She showed him to Scott's room.

As she walked Clint back to the door, holding her robe tightly closed around her thin frame, she said, "I don't allow no whiskey in the rooms. Am I gonna have a problem with him?"

"I don't think so," Clint said. "Give him some slack, his new business burned down tonight."

"Oh my," she said. "That's terrible. What will he do?"

"He's going to rebuild it."

At the door she asked, "Will he be able to pay his rent?"

"He will," Clint said. "You don't have to worry about that, either."

As he started down the steps she called out, "Are you sure you wouldn't like to stay for some . . . coffee?"

"I would," he said, "but I'm afraid it's past my bed time. How about another time?"

"Sure," she said, "Another time." And closed the door.

***

Gina brought Vanessa over to Napier's table, and he looked at them in surprise.

"I thought you should talk to her," Gina said. "She has somethin' to tell you."

"Well, all right, then," Napier said. "You can go." He looked at Vanessa. "Sit."

She sat, not as nervously as Gina had. She knew that with Tess gone, Napier was going to need a new top lady. Maybe she could convince him to choose her.

"You spent some time with the Gunsmith," he said.

"Until I figured out who he was and what he wanted," she said.

"And what was that?"

"You," she said. "He asked me all kinds of questions about you and Tess."

"What about Tess?"

"He said he's tryin' to find out who killed her," she said. "I don't know why he was askin' about you. He said he thought you might have some information for him."

"Did he, now," he said. "And what else did you tell him?"

"Nothin'," she said. "I didn't tell him nothin'."

He studied her for a moment, then said, "All right, go back to work."

"I did tell him one thing."

"What's that?"

"That you weren't my pimp."

"Why'd you tell him that?"

"I didn't want him to think I was coverin' for you, or anythin'."

"What made you think I needed to be covered for?" Napier asked her.

"I dunno," she said. "I just didn't really wanna cooperate with him, ya know?"

"Okay," Napier said. "You're a smart girl."

She grinned at that, and went off to finish her night's work.

He went back to drinking, and planning.

Chapter Forty-Four

When Clint got to his hotel he was ready for a night's sleep, a bath in the morning and then breakfast. He hoped, after all that, he'd have a solution to the Napier problem. Or maybe, something would come to hin and the sheriff after they talked to Mitchum, the bartender.

However, when he reached the hotel he had changed the order of things. He decided to have the bath first, and then go to bed. He stopped at the front desk to arrange for the tub, then went to his room to wait for it to be ready. As he removed his shirt he could smell the smoke that was still on it. In the morning he would have to buy a couple of newer ones. The jeans also smelled, but they were already pretty new. He decided just to let them air out, or perhaps there was a Chinese laundry in town that could refresh them for him. Perhaps Tyson would know—or Hallie.

He was thinking about Halie when there was a knock at his door. Thinking it might be her, he nevertheless answered the door with his gun in his hand. It was the hotel clerk.

"Uh, just wanted to let you know your bath is ready, sir," the young man said.

"Thank you," he said. "I'll be right down."

He went down, taking a fresh shirt and a towel from the room. When he got there he found a steaming hot tub, and a couple of fresh towels on a chair next to it. He put his gunbelt on the towels, and slipped into the tub.

***

Napier had come to a decision.

There was no use waiting any longer. Tonight was the time to get rid of the Gunsmith, even if he had to slip into his room and cut his throat.

That would probably be better than setting the entire hotel on fire.

Although that was very tempting.

***

When Hallie got to Clint's hotel she went to the desk clerk and asked if he was in.

"He is, Ma'am," the young clerk said, "but right now he's havin' a bath."

"Really?" she asked. "And where is that?"

Wordlessly, the clerk pointed . . .

***

Napier saw the woman entering the hotel ahead of him, and waited until she finished her business with the desk clerk. Then he went in. The lobby was empty but for him and the clerk. He closed the front doors of the hotel, and locked them. Then walked to the front desk, reaching into his pocket.

"Hey, Mister," the clerk said, "you can't close them doors . . ."

When the door to the room opened Clint reached for his gun, but relaxed when he saw it was Hallie.

"How did you know where I was?"

She closed the door, put her back to it and folded her arms across her chest.

"I asked."

"And he told you?"

She smiled prettily.

"He pointed," she said.

She had changed from the dress she usually wore at work, was wearing a shirt and trousers. Her hands went to the neck and started to unbutton.

"What are you doing?" he asked.

"I suddenly need a bath," she said. "That tub looks big enough. "Do you mind?"

"Hell, no."

She got herself naked, then walked to the tub and stepped in. Clint shifted so she could sit opposite him. The nipples of her pert little breasts pointed right at him.

"Can I have the soap?" she asked.

He started to pass her the bar of soap, then dropped it into the water between them.

"Oops," he said.

"I'll get it."

She reached into the water and got ahold of his hard cock. She tugged on it, then began to stroke it. Eventually, it popped up out of the water.

She moved forward, gliding onto his thighs, and into his lap. She kissed him deeply, and lifted her hips so the head of his cock could poke at her wet pussy. When she slid down on him her eyes went wide and she let out a sigh.

"Damn," he said, and they began to move together. She started to bounce up and down on him so hard they were spilling water from the tub to the floor. There was nothing subtle about the intention, here. She went faster and faster and finally, as he felt her body tremble, she muffled a scream by biting him on the shoulder.

"Ow," he said, and suddenly began to spurt inside of her.

That was when they heard the scream.

Chapter Forty-Five

"What was that?" she asked, her eyes wide.

"I'll go and see."

He eased her off of himself and got out of the tub. She followed. He hurriedly dried himself, got dressed, and took his gun from his holster.

"Stay here," he said, as he dressed. "Keep the door closed."

"Does it lock?" she asked.

He looked at it.

"No. Take that wooden chair and shove it under the doorknob after I go out. Kick it, so it's tight."

"Okay. Be careful."

"I will."

He opened the door and stepped into the hall, waited to hear her shove the chair into the door, then walked down toward the front desk.

When he got there, he saw a few people on the stairs, coming down from the second level. None of them were dressed.

"Go back upstairs and stay in your rooms," he told them. When they didn't move fast enough he showed them his gun. "Now!"

The men and women on the stairs turned and ran back up. That was the first time Clint peered behind the desk. The young clerk was on the floor in a pool of blood that was originating from a huge wound on his neck. It had to be he who had screamed.

He went to the front doors of the hotel and found them locked from the inside.

The Butcher of the Bayou was in the hotel, somewhere.

Hallie put her ear to the door, but couldn't hear anything on the other side. She considered taking the chair away and opening it to have a look, but decided against it. Then, as she was flip-flopping again on the idea, there was a knock at the door.

"Yes?" she said, her voice quivering.

***

Clint looked back down the hall, the way he had come. Was there a way for the Butcher—Napier—to have gotten behind him? If the man got ahold of Hallie, it would be all over.

He went back down the hall to the closed door and knocked.

"Yes?" he heard her say.

"It's Clint. Are you all right?"

"Yes, I'm fine. What's going on?"

"Just stay in there, Hallie," he said. "And don't open the door unless you're sure it's me."

"A-all right."

He went back to the lobby, satisfied that she was safe—for now.

Chapter Forty-Six

Where was he?

What were the chances he'd killed the desk clerk, and left? Not good. The cut on the clerk was too simple, too clean. The Butcher wouldn't be satisfied with that. But then, the clerk wasn't his target, was he?

Clint felt the man was there to kill him, pure and simple. One of them was going to put an end to the other one on this night. If Napier killed Clint, he could go on with his reign of madness. If Clint killed him, he could leave town and try to put this all behind him.

Clint had dressed quickly, out of the bath. He was barefoot, had his gun in his hand. His boots and holster were still on a chair by the tub. He was wearing his shirt and jeans, and he felt damp inside his clothes.

He scanned the lobby with his eyes. The only other egress from there was the dining room, which was closed now. Or Napier had gone upstairs, to the second floor. But if he had done that, he would have run into the people who had come down.

So that made it the dining room.

Clint walked to the entrance and looked into the dark interior. He'd eaten there a few times, but did not remember where the lamps were.

He looked around the lobby, again. The lamps on the wall were oil lamps. He went over to one to see if it would come off the wall so he could take it into the dining room with him, but they were affixed firmly.

He went back to the entrance. All he could do was wait until his eyes adjusted—but he wondered how many other ways out of the dining room there were? Certainly the kitchen.

The chairs were piled up on top of the tables. Napier could have been behind any of them, or in the kitchen, waiting. He could see Clint, perfectly backlit by the light in the lobby.

But he finally had to do it. Take a step into the dining room, and then another, careful that Napier wasn't waiting just inside. Too late he thought he should have grabbed one of the guests on the stairs and sent them for the sheriff.

He was inside the dining room, now. He stopped to listen. Maybe he would hear Napier breathing, or moving. But there was nothing. If he was gone this was all for nothing, but somehow he didn't think that was the case.

"Come on, Napier," he said. "This is supposed to be between you and me, remember?" He waited for an answer, but none came. "Why'd you have to kill that kid behind the desk?"

Still no answer.

"So this is your plan? Jump out at me in the dark? Like a ghost? Or a coward?"

Trying to goad him didn't seem to work.

"Okay, I know you're not a coward." But he tried again. "You're just crazy."

He took a few more steps. The shaft of light from the doorway created all these shadows on both sides. Napier could easily have been hidden there. The kitchen was directly across from Clint. It had double swinging doors, which he could make out in the lobby light.

Then he got it. He had a gun in his hand and, more than likely, Napier just had his razor. He had never seen the man with a gun. Now he wished he had his .32 New Line tucked in the back of his belt.

"I tell you what, Napier," he said. "I'll put my gun down. Then it'll be you, me, and your razor."

That really wasn't a good idea. The last time he had tangled with Napier he hadn't done real well. He hadn't even been able to get his gun out. The man was quick with that razor. But nothing was happening, and he felt the need to force it, get it done.

Finish it.

"I'm putting the gun down, Napier," Clint said. "Over here, on one of the tables."

"Not on the table," Napier's voice said.

It was clear, so he wasn't in the kitchen.

"Then where?" Clint asked, because he wanted the man to speak again.

"Toss it out into the lobby," Napier's voice said.

Left side of the room, in the shadows.

Clint changed his mind. He needed to do something that would light up that side of the room.

"You know what, Napier?" he said. "I don't think so."

"Adams—"

"You're trapped," Clint said. "You made a big mistake coming here, probably thought you were unbeatable. Is that it?"

"You can't take me, Adams," Napier said. "And you can't shoot me. I'm not armed."

"You've got a razor."

Clint heard something clatter out on the floor of the lobby.

"Now I don't have a razor," Napier said. "Get rid of the gun and we'll do this man-to-man."

"Before we could do that," Clint said, "I'd have to find another man."

He pointed the gun in the direction of Napier's voice and pulled the trigger two times. He knew he wouldn't hit him, but the muzzle flashes lit the room and he saw which table-and-chair setup Napier was hiding behind.

In fact, in the muzzle flash of the second shot he saw Napier coming at him with a crazed look in his eyes—and a razor!

He fired twice. He knew the lead hit its mark, but Napier still ran into him, slashing with the razor.

Chapter Forty-Seven

"What was he thinkin'?" Sheriff Tyson wondered.

"He wanted to get rid of me," Clint sad. "Get it over with, and then move on with his craziness. Even as he died he ran into me and tried to cut me."

Tyson looked down at the body on the floor of the dining room. The lamps had been lit. There were people in the lobby, guests who had been awakened by the shots. Clint had sent one of them for the sheriff.

"Was he crazy?"

"He charged me with a razor while I was holding a gun," Clint said. "What do you think?"

"I thought you said he tossed the razor into the lobby."

Clint crooked his finger at the lawman and walked him out to the lobby. When he pointed to the floor the sheriff looked and saw an almost harmless whittling knife.

"Well," Tyson said, "you shot a man who was tryin' to kill you. And who killed the desk clerk. And who probably was the Butcher of the Bayou. I ain't gonna hold you."

"Good," Clint said, "I'm leaving town tomorrow."

"What about your friend?"

"He'll be fine," Clint said. "He'll have my money to re-build with. There is one thing, though."

"What's that?"

"The bartender at Cajun Charlie's."

"Mitchum?"

"Keep an eye on him," Clint said. "I still think they were connected, somehow."

"You sure you don't wanna stay and check it out?"

"No," Clint said. "I'm leaving that up to you."

"Don't wanna tell me how to do my job, huh?"

"Not really," Clint said, "but if I was going to say something . . ."

"Yeah?"

". . . I'd recommend you hire a couple of real deputies."

"That might not be a bad idea," Tyson said.

"And now I'm going to go upstairs to my room and try to get some sleep. Maybe you can get all these people to go back to theirs and keep quiet."

"I'll try."

"And maybe get the owner to put another clerk behind the desk."

"Got it. Is there any thin' else?"

"I don't think so."

At that moment they both heard a girl's voice calling "Clint! Clint, are you all right?"

"Oh yeah," Clint said, "there's a girl in a room at the end of that hall, you might want to tell her—you know what? Never mind. I'll do it myself."

Coming Soon!

THE GUNSMITH
435
The Ghost of Butler's Gulch

For more information
visit: www.speakingvolumes.us

Coming Spring 2018

Lady Gunsmith 5
The Portrait of Gavin Doyle

For more information
visit: www.speakingvolumes.us

On Sale Now!

THE GUNSMITH
432
The Bank Job

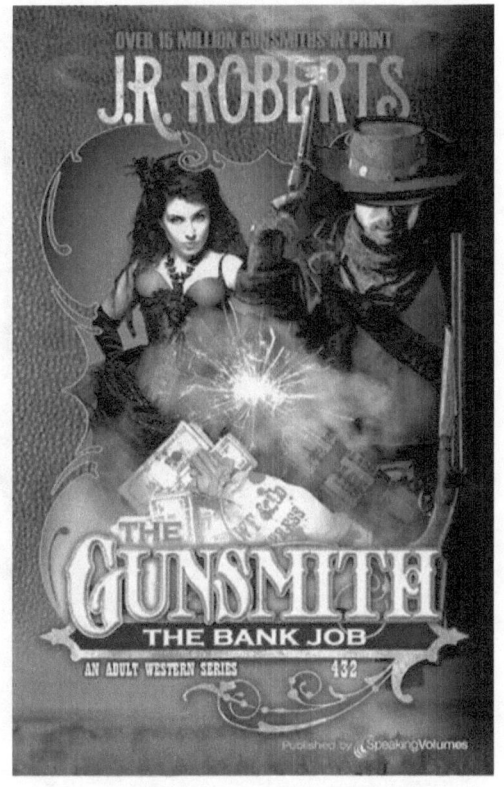

For more information
visit: www.speakingvolumes.us

On Sale Now!

THE GUNSMITH
431
The Science of Death

For more information
visit: www.speakingvolumes.us

On Sale Now!

THE GUNSMITH
430
Show Girl

For more information
visit: www.speakingvolumes.us

On Sale Now!

MOUNTAIN JACK PIKE *series*
by
Award-Winning Author
Robert J. Randisi (J.R. Roberts)

For more information
visit: www.speakingvolumes.us

www.ingramcontent.com/pod-product-compliance
Lightning Source LLC
Chambersburg PA
CBHW030452250626
47154CB00003BA/1243